Halloween

BEN GREER

Halloween

MACMILLAN PUBLISHING CO., INC.

New York

Macmillan Publishing Co., Inc.
866 Third Avenue, New York, N.Y. 10022
Collier Macmillan Canada, Ltd.

Library of Congress Cataloging in Publication Data

Greer, Ben.
    Halloween.

    I. Title.
PZ4.G8156Hal   [PS3557.R399]   813'.5'4   78-15065
ISBN 0-02-545510-9

First Printing 1978

Printed in the United States of America

For George and Susan Garrett

Children of the same family, the same blood, with the same first associations and habits, have some means of enjoyment in their power which no subsequent connections can supply.

—Jane Austen, *Mansfield Park*

Whoever fights monsters should see to it that in the process he does not become a monster.

—Nietzsche, *Beyond Good and Evil*

Part One

He had never laughed over her bones. The dead had their rights. In the woods he had his manners down.

Raphael stuck a new clove into his bad tooth. His mouth sweetened. The pain faded. He stretched out his legs on the sand and pine needles. The trees were silent over him. He could hear cars going into the city. Evening traffic. He touched the top of her skull. Dry bone, smooth bone. She still had some yellow braids. A lot was rotted, but she still had a little hair. He had killed her just after he left the asylum. Two months ago. He had put some plastic over the top part of her and planted some marigolds to keep the bugs away.

3

When he found out that Patra Lee did not love him, he slit open her esophagus. He stuffed her into the stump hole. Now he came two or three days a week. Here was his dead love. Love rotting in braids. He had killed Patra Lee by the book. A neat job. Simple, clean work. Raphael pulled the small notebook from his jeans: pasted-in pictures of dissection from Gray's Anatomy. He traced a finger along the dotted line of the lower bowel. Colostomy.

Raphael looked out toward the city. He could see Koose-watchi bridge and bright car lights. The trolley-car tracks lay just to the side of the bridge. The Pasques always rode the trolleys. They were so dramatic.

He was going to cut open Jess Pasque's bowels tonight. The tissue there was very soft. He had started working for the Pasque family one month ago. He was what they called a Birddog: a debit collector. Cross Pasque had employed him. Cross trusted him.

Tonight Raphael would be opening up his boss's sister. Bowels didn't smell so bad.

Raphael stood up. He pulled the piece of plastic over Patra Lee. He slipped his notebook back into his jeans and began moving toward the city. He had heard Blake had come to town. Raphael would cut up anyone he had to and just set them in the woods to visit.

"I'm coming," he said out loud. It was only fair. He chuckled a little going through the briers.

"I'm coming for you now."

To be born into a family of actors reduced your chances out there. They liked to keep you on their stage. They always wanted you back. But his mother was at last prepared to leave them tonight. Now Blake could begin the quest.

He rubbed his thumb across the wooden match box. A hunt scene engraved in satin wood. Hounds in pursuit of the laughing fox. It was a family present and now full of downers and antibiotics. Treasure. He took one Valium, two ampicillin, and swallowed some bourbon. Whiskey was bitter. He settled back into the cool chair and the hotel ferns. He watched her move gracefully beyond the marsh and white sand.

At a distance they always seemed more lovely. Close to them you could see where the salt water took away from their beauty. But from here the ship was cutting across the sea on a fine course, from her waterline up proud in flawless white, her masts brown and the sails upon them working and full and blue. She came about and turned into the evening mist of the sea.

In the marsh below the beach, the water moved smoothly. The tide was brown and going out. The first line of marsh grass faded from green to violet. Beneath palmettos a few cranes hunted fiddler crabs. The long piers were clean. The night lamps stood rusting and red in the white sun of the coast.

Blake felt apprehensive about being home again. He had called Alfbender twenty minutes ago. The lawyer would be here soon. He touched his forehead. The fever was up. He felt lonesome and looked around the bar for some conversation. He needed to talk about nothing. He needed a stranger and polite words to pass the time.

Two golfers threw down some peanuts and drifted out talking putters. The rest of the tables were empty. No music played. Blake looked hopefully toward the bartender. He was a crew-cut man. Rosy-faced and short. He wore a white shirt and yellow bow tie and looked like a doughnut baker.

Blake moved quietly toward the bar. His legs ached from fever. "Could I have a little more soda?

"I make them pretty strong, huh?"

"My stomach's hurting. You know anything about ampicillin?"

"Probably shouldn't drink with it. You look red. You sick?"

"Mono."

"No kidding?"

6

"Yep."

"You really got mono?"

Blake looked at him. "Yeah, I got it."

"What's your liver doing?"

"It's not in my liver."

"Oh, yes it is. Damn straight it is. You keep walking around and she'll swell up on you. I'm telling you livers do that." He poured some soda.

Blake nodded at the bartender's tie hoping to turn things around. "Hey, I like your yellow bow tie."

"It's just about the color of your eyes."

"I'm okay."

"If your liver goes you're dead. There ain't no replacements."

"Right."

"If they could find something to take up the slack of the liver we'd be alright. Why, we'd all live forever. Maybe you should be home in bed."

"I'm headed that way."

"What's your name?"

"Pasque."

"No kin to Jess Pasque?"

"My mother."

The bartender propped his face in his hands. "Really?"

Blake glanced back at the quiet table.

"I listen to her twice a week. She's got the best radio show in the state. That's one funny woman. I used to listen to your dad, too." He dropped his eyes respectfully. "Must be nice to come from such a prestigious family."

They were a cage of butterflies. Beautiful and cloistered. His father, Cross and Millis and Jess had all tried the outside. But the world gave applause grudgingly, and they had retired to their own games and regal egos. They were a family of monarchs.

"Thanks for the soda," Blake said.

"You say hello to your folks for me. Tell them I'm a fan."

Blake sat back down at his table. He was just a fan too. Nothing more. He was not coming home to stay. He was going to get a job with Las Piltes shipping line. They said something about needing seaman's papers. He would get those. He knew there would be no trouble shipping out, because he had started now. He had left the university. At last he had begun.

Lately Blake had dreamed of being out on the ship. The dream was not a charmer. Always he found himself walking the deck bemused and a little frightened by all the rigging above him. Suddenly the ship would run aground, not into rock or sand, but rather packing into a coast of morning glories, yellow and pink and banked high as the masts. A tall man approached him.

"You're to be hanged," the captain said.

Gold medals rattled on him and Blake could smell fruit on his white shirt. "Right," he said.

"My man is coming," the captain said and put his hand on his black revolver.

"Let me hold the gun," Blake said.

"My man is coming."

"Look," said Blake and went down on both knees and kissed the toe of the captain, then grabbed his ankles and threw him. Quickly he scooped up the gun and was off the ship and wading through the morning glories. He stopped. The captain was standing on the deck in brilliant sunlight. Blake lowered the pistol and shot, and half the man's skull blew off. Yellow dust glittered into the air as his body dropped into the blooms below the ship. In a white room, eating fresh kibbe and sipping lime juice, Blake found himself listening to a radio which announced the murder. How good he felt at having them after him. How fine the food tasted and how perfectly neat the butt of the revolver felt in his hand.

He looked at the bar clock. Six-thirty. Where was Alfbender? Up to no good? His Uncle Cross had used the lawyer more than once to commit Jess to the asylum. Blake had to seek out Alfbender's position first. He needed somebody to trust tonight. If Jess sincerely wanted to leave town, then his uncle and aunt would sincerely fight to keep her. He sipped his drink. The whiskey was like a sword in this matter. It gave him edge and power.

The first day back in town he had used for walking. He had forgotten how much a city could be in you, as he wandered down the street of ancient houses, life still noisily stacked inside them, though the wooden structures themselves were coming apart at the porches and roofs now. He paused by the spavined groceries where he had swigged soft drinks full of peanuts as a boy and listened to the banter of the old Chinamen whose names he never learned still standing before their dragon doors, picking their teeth with fishbacks, the air about them ripe from the smell of fresh shrimp. And he had moved between the spaces of those houses farther into town and of better money, whose doors were fringed with stained glass and wrought iron, the gardens between them green and alive with oleander and jasmine beneath clashing palms and banana trees. Later he went down to Pinkey's for the sixty-cent beer. He traded a few jokes with the fishermen, though they were not so much fun. There was talk about the strange killing of animals in the town. In the evening Blake took the trolley to the beach. He walked between the dunes. He remembered the blue veins of his father's forearms fresh and full.

The telegram had been to the point:

BLAKE. FOUND YOUR FATHER AT SIX A.M.
PLEASE COME HOME. LOVE MAMA.

He had not been able to return home until the next day. His father had already been buried. He had never seen him scrubbed and suited and asleep in the box. His face clean and

9

shaven of life. He had not been given the gift of his father's dead face.

After his father's death Jess sank into booze and pills again. She slipped into Millis's kindergarten class and threw a moon at the kids. Cross gave the usual bribe to the usual magistrate, and they carted Jess off to State Hospital for a month's stay. Blake was not allowed to visit her there. He returned to school. He worried about his mother. He grieved for his father and felt that the rest of the family was keeping a secret about his death.

He continued his first semester in college and found that in real life—that is, life beyond the eyes of your family—the world was a wondrous, trafficking place. People kissed in public, hundreds had no established bedtimes, all were concerned that their clothes fit exactly and their socks matched. For Blake, it was a new world.

In those first days of school he felt very shy and left his rooming house only for class. Finally he summoned courage and went out to the Pink Flamingo diner. Blake was surprised to see all the students eating there. He had thought college kids did not eat a real breakfast. He thought they stoked themselves with beer and soda crackers in the morning. He felt better seeing them here and stated very clearly to himself that *he* was a college kid now, though he still did not really believe so. Sitting in his booth, trembling and trying to drink his coffee black (like the others), he found himself looking at those about him in wonder. The students all looked so fine and sure in their blue jeans and flannel shirts. They moved in a marvelous way. They had blond hair and faultless blue eyes. When Blake caught his own reflection in the glass doors of the phone booth he felt ashamed of the skinny body and freckles. He wore a crew cut and had uneven teeth. Those around him were as confident as television ads. Some were so bold they didn't shave.

As he stood at the cash register to pay for his meal, he

remembered his father's advice: Always pay by check. He had gotten the special: one egg and grits—thirty-eight cents. He started to fill out the check and then suddenly forgot the name of the diner. Casually he looked around: No signs. He began to shake a little and knew he was blinking a lot. The cashier leaned against the counter and lowered his pepper eyes at him. He had stitches in his chin and no smile. The line behind Blake was grumbling. He finally spotted a ticket and printed in "Pink Flamingo." Then the realization came clattering: he had never written out a check for under a dollar. He didn't know how. The blood shot from his heart to his face. He tried to talk himself cool.

"Thirty-eight cents, huh?" he said, trying to move his head languidly to the left as if examining his check stub.

"That's above thirty-seven and below thirty-nine," the cashier said.

"You know us English majors," Blake said. His smile wouldn't work.

The cashier narrowed his eyes and pried a little finger toward his back teeth.

How in hell did you write a thirty-eight-cent check? Blake tapped his pen as if something was wrong with it. His belly was jumping now. "Lousy pen."

"Huh?"

"Nothing," Blake said. The mumbling behind him grew rougher. Across the street, bells were ringing in the classrooms.

Blake scribbled out thirty-eight, stuck the check into the cashier's hand, and made the door.

"Hey! This is for thirty-eight dollars, bud!"

"Keep it. Just keep it," Blake yelled and rushed into the street.

In the next few weeks Blake let his hair grow. In 1968 everyone was marching. Though he had not yet defined it, the first need for the quest had flashed through him.

Something tagged him at his neck, brought him out of the daydream. Blake turned. Alfbender was slouched and smiling behind him.

"Hurray. You're back," Alfbender said.

Blake used his manners. He shook the lawyer's hand. "I'm just having a little drink here."

"Before it all begins?"

"Look, do you think Mother really wants to leave?"

"Let me cop a buzz." Alfbender waved at the bartender. Four or five rings sparkled on his fingers. His hair lay in oily strands about his neck and yellowed his collar. He was wearing a black suit and a red silk bow. His face was gray and square and slightly pocked.

Blake had known him almost ten years. The fellow had eels for brains, though he was somewhat oddly musical. He often carried a harmonica or piccolo, which he played at spare moments. He had conspired with Cross a number of times and committed Jess to the State Hospital. Blake had to find out if the lawyer was working against her now, and he wanted his lines to sound right.

When his drink arrived Alfbender took a noisy swallow and wiped a long-nailed thumb across his mouth.

"Whose corner you in this round?" Blake asked. He had to sound—he had to *be* tough.

Alfbender grinned and pulled at his nose. "I'm lacing your gloves, sweetheart."

"Good." Blake studied his eyes. They checked out, for now.

"Jess left the house."

"She wrote me about it. That's why I'm here."

"She's serious about leaving the family."

"Okay."

"Says she's got a part in New York. Something off-Broadway, she says."

"Do you think that's true? I mean, it's not booze talk?"

"I think it's pretty straight."

Blake dipped a finger into his drink and stirred the ice. "Listen, I want to get her out. More than anything else, that's what I want to do."

"He's got his Birddogs out right now. Had them around the train and bus station for a week. Cross ain't taking his fingers out of the pie so easy."

"Who's Birddogging?"

"Two bums out of the company. Collect debits down in darky land. Twenty-five cents a week for coffins."

"If she's really got the will this time, we should get her out of town tonight."

"How lovely. On Halloween, too. Got your costume?"

"She's doing her Halloween show tonight?"

"Yeah. Down at the Swan. She's interviewing Winky and a couple of artists."

The Swan Theater lay fifteen blocks down on Boyston Street. Blake had performed there with his mother and father when he was a boy. Mostly little-theater productions. Occasionally Blake had acted in some of his father's plays.

Blake leaned over his drink. "One thing, Alf. I really do need your help tonight. I'm sick. Kind of weak. I just don't want to play any games."

"You and me are straight."

"You give me a lift to the Swan?"

Blake sat back in Alfbender's Nash and listened to the grumbling gears. Palmetto trees lined the road. Going away from the waterfront, you passed two-bit businesses and grimy fruit stands. The adjoining streets were mostly brick. The buildings wooden. Mildew and rusting porch fans. This part of town was not historical. Sherman had not camped here. Farther down still lay the squares of the city. Each square a park. Gabled houses rose above fountains. Stone lions trimmed in impeccable ivy reared before driveways. The two newly restored streetcars passed each other as if synchronized.

At school Blake had involved himself in antiwar demonstrations. One week he marched around in a circle with people who didn't bathe very often and to no one in particular shouted "Stop the bombing now." Another time he and fifty other students sat down to block a strategic administrative door. The faculty used the side entrance. The war simply had no meaning for him. No reality. However the expectation and anxiety grew in him that something was waiting— some fight or duty—and that he had only to find the avenue to it. In an afternoon English class while listening to a lecture on Spenser, the idea tapped him between the eyes: search to do something notable, something of merit. Strive to find a cause —a quest. Windmills in Spain, but he didn't care. He wanted to act, to do something.

Blake went to the Red Cross and asked to go overseas to work with disaster victims. The receptionist told him he didn't have enough education. To be a "good neighbor" you had to be a B.A. He signed up at the Presbyterian Center to visit old people at the Good Shepherd Nursing Home. He took his guitar and sang to two old ladies. They smiled. Blake felt better. Then the nurse told him they were both deaf. When he began "Silver Dagger" for his third patient, the old man started screaming. He threw his water pitcher. His swollen catheter bag burst. Blake grabbed his guitar and ran down the hall and heaved just two feet from the head nurse's station.

Meanwhile his Uncle Cross and Aunt Millis were calling him three or four times a week saying that his mother was "just going to pieces over the smallest things." Blake went to the infirmary and was given a prescription for Valium. Things moved a little slower but he still wanted to go somewhere, to be involved in something of worth. One morning he received his mother's letter saying that she *had* to leave the family, that they were monsters and she needed his help to start a new life. Blake took the letter as a sign, as the direction he had been looking for. To free his mother was his quest, or at least its first stage.

Alfbender stopped at a traffic light. The street lamps had switched on. The dark was settling fast.

"I'm going to let you off a couple corners up. I want to check on these Birddogs."

"I'm not worried about them."

"I got a feeling you should be. A feeling. And stay out of the alleys. Somebody's killing cats and dogs. Stringing them up. Some crazy."

Alfbender pulled through the light. Blake looked south. Pulaski Street led to the causeway and home.

Home stood one mile beyond the city and across the marsh on Cane Island. Blake was sure his aunt and uncle were already at work there. They would not let Jess go gently any time.

In his memory he saw Jess childishly, for it was mostly as a child that he had perceived her. He saw a tall woman who moved graciously in pleated dresses and high heels. She was beautiful. She could seem the elegance of the moon and the quiet of the last star or rail against the panes of other lives like a winter squall. She held forth against his father and tried to outwit him, though she usually lost. For years they clashed in long Shakespearean scenes, accusing one another of infidelities and schemes and coldness. At the end of these tableaux one always refused to sleep with the other, and they went to separate rooms in the great house called home. His mother pounded the walls. His father screamed out some well-constructed lament about how his genius was never upheld or embraced by those about him. When Blake was a boy the bouts had seemed horrible to him. He saw in his parent's eyes real rage, or so he believed. Later Jess told him that they had loved most of the frays and many times each had planned out the scenes. For his mother and father joy had always been found in mock violence. But in all of these dramas neither had intended actual pain. They had never drawn blood and laughed.

His Uncle Cross and Aunt Millis were quite different.

Millis was musical. She had wanted to be a concert pianist. She had tiny red hands which matched the color of her hair. Blake's grandmother had told Millis that her hands were far too small, her talent merely adequate. Nevertheless Millis graduated from Converse Conservatory and went out on an up-country tour. She played in three separate towns and quit. She became a grade-school music teacher. She never married and became fat. She developed a taste for her own misery, though she did not exclude her sister's. She was a lover of bitter chocolates.

Cross had never married either and had no use for music or the stage. If anything, he loomed as the dark man in the wings who knew well about absolute ends like the dropping of curtains and blacking of lights. He had used Birddogs against Jess twice before and had even threatened Blake's father with them. Blake did not believe Cross to be an evil man, a man who deliberately set traps and bound people because the suffering soothed him. But Blake knew that his uncle understood entirely what he needed to survive and that he would pull from anyone in the family those strengths that assured him a safe portion of life. In this way his formal preoccupation with Jess frightened Blake, for if the pain of need was great enough, the method for relief could always be tallied as the expense of peace.

One cold night when Blake was seven years old his uncle slipped into his room, turned up the gaslight, and raked the bedded coals of the fire across the new log. The noise of the sputtering wood awakened Blake. Cross stood in the gold gaslight cradling a cup of coffee. He had been outside. The cold rolled off his greatcoat like a breathing. He pulled Blake from the bed and swooped him into the greatcoat, holding him fast between his knees. The new log tattled and spat, and his uncle smelled of cigarettes as he peeled a fat apple and told Blake how sick his mother had become and that he needed his help. He fed Blake slivers of white apple and pushed the cup of bitter coffee to his lips. He dressed him and carried him out into the dark.

After the Birddogs lifted him into the ambulance and the harsh doors slammed, Blake felt his knees crouch and his hands reach out into the dimness toward anything that might hold him close. The engine cranked. The ambulance lunged forward and he saw Jess lying beneath the tight leather straps, her face drawn and lonely. A tube led from her arm to a bottle hanging above her. She saw him and spoke easily. She said not to be afraid. Her voice felt silver to him and she smelled of her own flat, brown odor which somehow brought comfort, though too the whiskey rode her breath. For a while they looked out the glass window of the roof and played big dipper and man in the moon and he tried to be brave in his heart though his chest hurt like something broken and his hands held himself tightly so he would not wet. He tried to keep his eyes on the stars and the surprised old moon and away from her wet eyes. The sorrowing eyes running with black mascara. The cramped hands that despite her quiet voice tore their skin against the manacles. He turned his face from the tube, which was dripping something into her veins. Something dark and rolling into the heart of his mother.

"Buckles, Mama loves you," Jess said.

He settled his hand on hers and felt her cold fingers twisting.

"Mama loves her little boy blue."

"I love you, Mama."

"You have the ambergris now? You didn't forget?"

Blake took the silver compact from his pocket and held it for her to see. "I snuck it out of your sweater. Nobody saw me. I was a jackrabbit."

"Just smooth it across my eyes now. Just easy rub it in."

The ambergris dissolved warmly between his fingers. He eased a palm onto her face. Delicately he traced the ambergris across her eyelids. The sweetness of the cream arose. He could feel the spheres, the beautiful lights moving warmly beneath his fingers.

"That's better, Buckles. That's a sweet baby." She opened her eyes and looked up at him from the mattress. "Pull the needle out, sonny."

"Cross said it makes your nerves not swell."

"They're going to do things to me now, aren't they?"

"They're helping, Mama."

"Don't let Mama go away down there and die."

"It's a hospital. It's got a swimming pool and big ole trees inside."

"What kind of trees?"

"Them sweetgum kind, I think. They got Coke machines, too."

"See Mama's arm? It hurts. They're shooting mud into the big blue vein."

"It's sleep, Mama."

"Pull it out, baby. It's some meanness in the night."

He could not look at her when she spoke to him now and her hands were jerking so hard. The mascara and ambergris melted down her cheeks. "Sleep now. I know. We'll play the night-night game. It'll make your nerves go away." He paused and then started off in the lilting, singsong voice she always used at night which brought him sleep. "E-v-e-r-y-b-o-d-y-'s g-o-n-e night-night. The moo cow's gone night-night and the big ole barn's gone night-night and the pecans way up in the trees gone way on to night-night too."

"Dirty, bad needle. They stuck it in my elbow. They rammed my bones."

She was beginning to writhe. The blanket kept slipping from her body, and he was afraid to put it back because he might touch her with no clothes on. "And the ole hooty owl has gone night-night and the bobwhite has long time ago gone night-night too."

18

"Oh, it hurts me."

"No, now. It's just the sandy man coming down in you."

"I can't see the moon."

"He's gone night-night. Why, the big ole moon's all rolled up in his covers, Mama."

The blanket fell away. He closed his face in his hands. He could hear her feet bucking against the manacles.

"It's a broken bottle stuck in my arm."

"Sleepytime," he said. The tears came down his face.

"Where am I going?"

"Rest now."

"Where is Mama going down to so fast, honey?"

"To rest is all."

"Nobody down here but me."

"The Lord's there, Mama. The Lord's with you in there."

"Hug me."

Blake felt his hands grinding together.

"Nighttime kiss," she said, the drug heavy in her voice. "Sweet snacktime now."

"You'll be alright now."

"Please hug Mama going far away so by herself."

He circled his arms around her neck and felt her breasts against him. He shuddered.

"Take it out of me . . . so far down. The dark is . . . so lonesome."

She was becoming quiet. "He's in there. The Lord."

"Not for me, no."

"Now I lay me down to sleep—"

"He's not in here . . . in way down here."

"I pray the Lord my soul to keep."

"I can't see. No, no. I got no light . . . and they . . ." Her voice went away to mumbles.

"If I should die before I wake, I pray the Lord my soul to take."

He laid his face on her neck and repeated this many times

19

until they passed into the gates of the asylum and the driver pulled him away. Another man came and they lifted Jess out of the ambulance. The October wind was mean and cold and blowing the black leaves. The two men peeped under the blanket and one let go a small whistle and they whispered together. Blake sat on the ground and felt the rage in him. The Birddogs climbed out of their car. They had followed all the way. He could hear the dimes ringing in their pockets. He watched the hospital men roll her into the elevator. They closed the screeching door and took her up into the strange-smelling building. He kept saying very softly above the silver dimes of the Birddogs and the laughter of the men in the dark with his mother and the black wind: "I love you. I love you. I love you, Mama."

Alfbender let him off near the first of the downtown squares.

"Meet you at the Swan," Blake said.

Alfbender looked about the square. "You keep under the streetlights. Out of the dark."

Blake nodded. The car's gears grated into the night.

The Swan was only four blocks down. Blake had not been back for some time. On the stoops of the big houses around the square the first jack-o'-lanterns were glowing. Paper skeletons and monsters shimmered in the windows of the blue row houses. Two early trick-or-treaters rattled huge grocery bags.

"Hope you get lots of candy," Blake said.

"Screw you, mother," said a skeleton.

Kind words were hard to find.

He did not feel a lot of hope in seeing Jess again. Would she be high on pills or booze or acid? He smiled a bit when he felt the Valium working in his jaw.

Just before the Swan stood a gurgling iron fountain which rose almost thirty feet into the night. Two lights shone on it from the surrounding boxwoods and revealed scores of dark-eyed and prancing stallions, just by them larger and almost frightening swans, and toward the top of the fountain hollow-eyed cherubs blowing water from their trumpets. The top of the fountain was capped by a statue of Aphrodite. She was made of stone and exquisitely held the first moonlight along the length of her legs and the smoothness of her arms and neck. Two masks held in her right hand were glowing above the water. As a boy Blake often looked out of the Swan's windows and, seeing the statue, thought perhaps someone had built the entire fountain to honor Jess, for the figure looked so much like her. When he told Jess how the statue's beauty seemed so like her own, she hugged him and then explained the myth of Aphrodite. At the end of the story Jess said that his grandmother had possessed this same kind of spelling beauty. Blake had seen the old pictures of her. She was Black Irish from County Leitrim. Her hair was dark as a starless night, her eyes black as inkwells. Her neck and hands called her lady and graceful and beguiling. She had arrived in Port Sound to become a teacher. She had ambition and her mind was tough and surprising. Jess had told him that men cooed and plotted over her and that they were not men of the red-handed wharves or the sea but ample-bellied fellows in silk vests and chiming watches, the wearers of engraved cuff links and morning-star stickpins and whiskers blown out to the sides of their faces. Katherine Speer had been wary of her beauty, a beauty that was so successful, so full and wonderfully made, that she even sat in the lower part of the church to keep the men from creaking their starched collars as she passed by or dropping their change noisily upon the floor in order to swivel around and gamble a wink. Two years after her arrival she courted and married Whitney Pasque—a bantam man with one bad lung, two stricken legs, and four rosy-colored fishing sloops. She brewed his tea and they had their kids and Whitney Pasque died leaving money in the bank. Blake's grandmother turned her mind toward simple math then. She sold her old crew and bought another, this one of salesmen and bookkeepers—life insurance. She raised her company and her children. She instilled in both one prime maxim: "Acorns 'is' diamonds in your own backyard."

Katherine Pasque had been a woman of mirrors and concern. She dreamed upon her image not in reckless vanity but rather as if she were storing the liveliness of her eyes and the radiance of her cheeks in dread of some coming and entire deprivation when none could find her beautiful and she on that account would lose the fascination with her existence. Her beauty did much more than sustain her, it sculpted an essential spirit of vivacity and resilience and pronounced her of value beyond any prestige that her success or her finely built house could acquire. Her beauty was her life.

Blake had feared his grandmother in the first of his life. She seemed to him severe and desolate. He remembered her as a woman at peace only when her family sat near. To Blake his aunt and uncle loitered about her, their hearts suppliantly ticking like small watches arranged about a great clock—all managing to record time but just faintly, their mechanisms barely touching against the metal of existence. Katherine Pasque tucked her children neatly into herself. She knew how to sort through every care and joy of her family, and if anyone was struggling in either too much joy or too much sorrow, she pulled them into herself and relieved them of excess. By emptying out each child and supplying the necessary supports, she balanced out her household and embroidered each of her children more securely into her own life.

Laid out before her mirror, dressed in perfect lace, her silvery hair brushed down her shoulders, Katherine Pasque expired at eighty-five after a harsh year of desolation and dye.

Raphael stood in the phone booth to the left of the fountain. He watched Blake. What was Blake thinking about?

How do brains work? Electricity? The brain is bicameral.
He had learned that from Valànce. His friend in the hospital.
Valànce the dam poisoner. Name the parts: cerebellum,
cerebrum, medulla oblongata. The cerebrum was what
Raphael would like to fool with on Blake. It reminded him of
cereal. Crunch, crunch. The cerebrum. Yeah, Blake was a
brains job, but not Jess. She was bowel. If Raphael had to go
after Blake, he'd just take out his little book and go on into
Blake's cerebrum. Raphael felt his mouth fill with saliva as
Blake walked past him. The lean white face. Soft olive
eyes. Lots of bones in him, though. Lots. Raphael dropped
the dime, called Thaggart, and told him to be at the Swan.
He had Blake figured.

Raphael waved at Blake's back, then stepped toward Madi-
son Square. He had to do something.

They were fairly tame now. They had been out of the zoo
a couple of months and people fed them. One was sleeping
six feet up on the live oak. It never heard Raphael. Maybe the
fountain made too much noise and didn't give it a chance.
Raphael got his fingers right under the tough little bones of
the throat. It gasped and kicked. Shush now, Raphael said.
He took it behind the fountain. He wanted to open his book
and check out an incision, but the creature was almost
scratching through his jacket now. He flipped out his razor.
Sized up the new-filed point. He went in below the sternum.
A little squeal. Where were the Isles of Langerhans? Now a
layer of fat. Cartilage. First blood. Deeper. The glimmer of
new blue bone. Then hard in now and smooth gliding down
through the intestines.

In the whole world there is no better feeling than sliding
from the sternum to the bladder.

The Swan Theater sat between a new loan company and
an old blood bank. The windows were covered in ivy and
wisteria and the sweetness of the blooming filled the streets.

The building had once had four floors. All but the first had been torn out so that when you walked in there rushed toward you the feeling of darkness and lean stars and space open and long as a tidal pool.

Blake pushed open the cool leather door. The theater smelled strongly of fruit: oranges and lemons and fresh melon. A brassy band was playing blues beneath the stage, and beside the band, set off from tables and chairs by a row of cotton bales, the bartenders were squeezing and straining fruits for drinks. He moved toward a table. Behind him a copper caldron simmered oyster stew. The band's music began to go down a little and Blake looked around. As usual the city's artists were here. A few wore costumes. They came mostly for the fancy drinks and the stew, the sawdust floor and the glass panes of the roof that allowed in the stars and out the thin trails of hashish.

Jess of course sat on the stage. As usual she was doing her show live. She liked the danger of it. She wore a pleated skirt and fatigue blouse open to the center of her chest. Her blond hair was pinned into an elegant bun and she wore a green mask across her eyes. She interviewed Winky Timlin (owner of the bar) about past times, past Halloweens, and all the celebrities whom he knew "personally." If Blake remembered correctly, Winky knew three stars: Pinky Lee, Sandra Dee, and Brenda Lee. Jess cued the Jamil Blues Band and they cranked up. Blake had arrived at the end of the thirty-minute show. The band was playing his mother's logo: the Skyliner theme. Jess waved the music down and signed off. "So now live from Winky's Swan Theater Lounge, this is Jess Pasque parting for now and saying—friends are always lovers in the dark."

Blake never quite understood this farewell, but Jess had used it for twenty years.

Jess cut off her equipment and stepped down from the stage. Blake stood and waved. She took off her mask, came over, and embraced him. She pushed him down into a chair, then girlishly giggled and sat very close beside him. "So kid. My little boy blue. What did you think?"

"Seemed like a good show, Mama. I got here late. But it seemed nice and all."

Her left eye winked at him. "Hey, hey!"

Blake paused, but he knew he couldn't deter her. "Whatdoyasay."

"Ice cream!"

"And we're a team." They rubbed noses and laughed.

Jess fussed at his collar. "You remember the Macon Fair? Every time at the Macon Fair we could knock them dead with that. You were four years old and sunlight dancing."

"They were a terrible audience."

"They were bright enough."

"They laughed because you were a great comedian."

"And your father said that at sixteen you could beat Olivier's Hamlet hands down."

Blake laughed at the exaggeration. At sixteen he had never even read Hamlet. But once again he found himself tempted to speak to his mother in a kind of dramatic dialogue that he had grown up using. There was a pattern of speech between him and his mother that was based on sound and flair and which often omitted sense for meter or effect. When he was younger he eased out onto his face and into the motions of his hands what his mother needed him to be: a reflection of herself, a congruent part which she could somehow be at ease with, talk to, love. This method of being came to him by birth, a deep and quiet channel of motion which he had naturally set out upon. In the rising and falling of masks upon his face, his mother and father had found initial comfort and he temporary worth.

But all of that had happened before the quest. Tonight he would start his life and so would she.

Blake slipped his hands into hers. "I hope you've got your stuff packed."

Jess withdrew her hands. "Hey, Rolly. Bring Mr. Buckles a little of the avocado punch."

The bartender glared back at her.

"That guy's got more crabs than the stew," she whispered. Pulling a cigar from her blouse pocket she lit up studying Blake.

"All you have to do is leave. Uncle Cross will never lock you up again. I promise."

Jess sat and puffed her cigar a little. Blake couldn't match her eye to eye. He never could. Somehow it seemed disrespectful, but he could see her face was changing some. The sharp oval chin was fuller. Tiny creases had begun in the hollowing of her cheeks. Her freckles seemed stronger.

"Tell me something," she said. "How's school?"

"Not so good."

"You're going to finish though."

"Nope. I'm not. I'm going on."

"You got some big ideas? You think you can change some things?"

"It sounds like every other kid. I know."

"Your father had big ideas. You know that."

"We're different."

"What are you going to do?"

"Lots of things. Good things. I'm on an adventure, Mama."

Jess put a hand on his neck, rubbed her thumb behind his ear. "Just remember your father. He was gutless. Even changed his name to mine because he said Pasque sounded better. He was a weak dreamer. Nothing more. You go ahead and quit school, but get something done. Now's the time. Tell me your plans."

"My plan is to get you out of here. You want out, don't you?"

Jess locked her hands behind her head and took a breath.

"Twenty years working this town and the towns down the line. Doing the big houses. Doing the little houses . . ."

She was singing.

"Doing the boys and doing the girls." She tossed a pill into the air and snapped it perfectly into her mouth. "Doing with hope and doing with dope." She swallowed. "And all of a sudden you get cornflakes for joints, the liver plays Camille, and your dear brother tries to fry your brains out. So you go on. You do a few one-acts but—it ain't so good, Mr. Buckles. It ain't so damn good."

To see her start flashing down the pills again depressed him, so he took out a couple more yellows for himself. Besides, the drinks were wearing off and the pills would help him glide. Still, he felt embarrassed hitting up in front of her. "Sorry," he said.

"You take what you need."

"So what was yours?"

"Vitamin C. I'm off the sinkers for now. You got bad news or something?"

"Birddogs."

The bartender brought the avocado punch.

"Tell me about it," Jess said.

"Alfbender says they're hanging around the bus station and airport."

"I don't know why they're at the airport. I'll never fly. But Cross does know."

"What?"

"Seven A.M. I'm booked on the rails for New York, if I get the part."

"When do you know?"

"The agent telegrams sometime tonight."

"Leave now. We can get on a bus outside town."

"Not without a 'for sure.' Not without a telegram. I don't need a cold room and a dead part. We can duck Cross 'til we hear. I know all the holes. I always beat him at hide and seek."

Blake sipped some juice. The telegram was for drama. He saw her eyes flicker and her lips smile around the cigar. He knew she both loved and feared this pursuit. He felt within himself too the old cleverness and arousal. To play with his family was straight adrenaline on a cloudy day. He took a larger sip of the spicy juice and puddled it under his tongue, then swallowed and sucked in the air just the way he had seen his father do in the beginning of such events. His throat and nose burned.

"What do you think Daddy would have said about your leaving?"

"At first he would support it. Then he would reject it. And finally he would cry and have some sort of colonic seizure."

"Daddy was crazy alright."

"Yes. A little mad."

"Maybe madness is an art."

"A craft, I fear, love."

"But he was a talented man. I mean he could have been something."

"Oh, he was a galaxy, and never should have sold out to radio and two-bit stages. My fault, you know. I broke him in the Big Apple. Back then I thought I was the great tragic heroine. Lady Macbeth come acalling."

Blake thought a moment. "There was something wrong in him. He couldn't step out into the world. He could never make his ideas work."

"Drink your juice, Buckles. I broke him. I really did. To Shepman of Broadway I said: 'You don't get the play if I don't get the lead.' "

Blake caught a movement to his right and saw Alfbender waving his arms, pointing toward the door. Two men stood near the entrance wearing bright red masks. They moved toward the bar.

When Blake turned to Jess he saw her hands suddenly reach for her chest. She rose a little from her chair, then fell to the floor. He knelt beside her.

"We got to get to the stage. Lib it. You follow?" she whispered.

A small crowd began forming around them.

Blake was trying to think of old lines. "Have you confessed?" he said, trying to muster a stage voice.

"*Mica, mica, parva stella,*" Jess said and began a loud coughing.

"Air!" Blake yelled. "She needs the element. Quick, get her to the stage."

Two or three people lifted her up. The red masks waited on the outside of the crowd. Blake scrambled onto the stage. "We're trapped?"

"Beneath," she said. "Lie down."

Jess was standing now, rolling up her sleeves. The crowd applauded. She held up a hand and turned to Blake, pale and stretched out on the stage.

"Noblest of men, would'st die? Hast thou no care of me?"

Blake kept silent.

"Here's sport indeed. How heavy weighs my lord!"

The crowd yelled "Boo!" Soup spoons and beer cans clattered onto the stage.

Jess signaled Alfbender. "Help, help, friends below." She pointed at the stage floor. Alfbender disappeared and the lights went out.

Blake felt the floor give underneath him and he was falling. He hit the mattresses hard. Jess dropped down behind him. A small light blinked beneath the stage. Blake could hear applause overhead. A side door opened.

"Hurry!" Alfbender whispered.

The street air hit Blake warm and steamy. He followed Alf and Jess down through the black alleys. He was moving too fast to look behind, but he listened carefully and heard nothing but their own feet on the gravel.

Moments later they were moving through the warehouse district. Broken streetlights, endless buildings and loading ramps. The murderous eyes of watchdogs.

Jess stopped quickly. "Safe?"

"As pie," Alfbender said, rolling his dead penny eyes.

"Sure," she said.

"Cross is taking this seriously, honey."

"See how he loves me."

"Yeah," Alfbender said.

"Maybe brother is ready to hit me up and stash me away again," Jess said.

"You're well now. You haven't hurt him," Blake said.

"I'm leaving home."

"Even Cross wouldn't use Birddogs on you when you are well."

"Just a little romp, maybe. Last digs."

"You should get on out of this city now," Alfbender said.

"No telegram, no movement. I can duck like a midget in a propeller factory."

Alfbender shrugged and walked a block ahead. Just across the street from a pawnshop he sat down and nearly sunk inside his baggy suit.

Above the pawnshop three faceted globes were whirling nacreous light. In the front window a clock read eight-fifteen. To the left of the shop ticked a towering electrical station surrounded by a chain-mail fence. As Blake followed Jess toward the shadows he looked behind him. Nothing. Ahead the gray cylinders were humming, and he could feel heat and smell static sparks and see by the safety lamps small and great wheels working and the vertebrae of ladders climbing into the dark.

Blake knew he should simply force her onto a bus. But the familial infection was spreading in him now: the need to play. He had all night really.

For Blake, Uncle Cross had always been a complete anomaly. While insurance lord and tyrant of actuaries and salesmen, he possessed, too, a scholarly nature, and knew particularly well the history of the Aztecs. But for the last fifteen years his obsession was his family. That it was small permitted him to learn all habits. He charted not only each relative's separate nature, but the collective soul that bound the family together as well. Using such knowledge, he pulled music from the wholeness of the family. Most times it bordered on cacophony and was strident and painful. At other moments he coached simple harmony. Cross was his mother's son. To prevail over such an uncle . . . Blake knew the dangers of even thinking of such a contest.

His gaze came back upon Jess standing awfully still before the electric plant, her white index finger signaling for him to come closer. Once beside her, he saw them.

Sitting small and puffed in the wire fence, all breathing and silent, splashed to blue and silver by the shop's globes, a large flock of sparrows huddled by the purring generators, so near that Blake could move two steps and touch them, though they rose above high and into the dark, toward the jack-o'-lantern moon.

"Now there's an audience," Blake whispered.

"Thousands," she returned. "How about this." Jess gave a short casual walk in front of the birds, then did a mime and silent fall.

Blake grinned, and Alfbender took out his piccolo and hit up a couple of mimicking notes for her.

Jess then began waving her arms about, feigning an oration. With a quick toss of her head, she silently tramped away, shoulders high and indignant. Once more she sprawled upon the ground. But this time as she rose, she glanced at Blake shyly like a young girl. She put a finger over her lips at him. From across the street Alfbender began playing a quiet melody.

She approached the birds slowly. Her hands moved delicately before her eyes as one leg gently raised itself and fell, and her arms grew into long twining branches like bare cottonwood winnowing against the starlight. She was dancing. Silent, pale, sorrowful as last light, before the rusting stairways and ranks of fuses, before the silent sparrows whose voices cried out in Jess's dream, whose eyes occasionally opened and flashed to watch her performance, then shuttered again and fell away to sleep.

She came to an end, arms coming to her sides in a graceful curve.

"Bravo," Blake whispered coming up behind her, the birds still motionless.

Jess was flushed and sweating. She still seemed beyond herself. "When I was a girl, I dreamed they preserved us. The birds, the animals. I dreamed that when I died one tiny bird swooped down and caught my soul and hid it away in the green forest. And all the other creatures tended and sang to me. They kept me and Mama and Daddy; they kept us all from the abyss."

She brushed at her nose then and toughened her voice. "Of course that was when I was a punk with pimples. Now in my grand sophistication I know that birds are simply birds, and the abyss is simply—nothing. Right?"

"We should keep on going," Blake said, scanning the square.

"We lost the creeps."

Blake gave her a handkerchief for the sweat about her face.

"Oh, I got Cross a few weeks ago. Did I tell you? I pucked him a good one." She folded the handkerchief into Blake's hands and kissed his knuckles.

"You should be more careful of him, Mama."

"Well, it was the night before the rally, and all through the stew, I stirred an emetic with a grin and a whew!" She wiggled her fingers beside her face. One eye closed and the other twinkled at him.

"Hello?" Blake said, not understanding.

"Your dear uncle had his yearly catfish stew rally to drum up money for his senators. I was mad at him for some reason and seeded the stew with Carter's little dribble pills. Oh, it cooked down good that night. Next day, great ladles of the potation having been consumed by guests and host alike, scores of them jumped up from their late brandy bellowing like boxcar beer pissers and cut the carpet for the jakes."

Alfbender collapsed into a tittering ball. The red bow trembled beneath his chin.

Laughing, Jess grabbed Blake and hugged him. He began to laugh too, seeing his uncle trying to approach the bathroom door, knees adroitly clipped together, attempting elegant little puffs at his cigarette.

Alfbender crossed the street and thumped the spit out of his piccolo. "Let's get on now."

"I need to go to the apartment. Come seven I want to be ready to hitch up." Jess opened a medallion around her neck. She rubbed the ambergris into her cheeks. "Let's haul it, Mr. Buckles."

They were away from the warehouses now and moving toward the river. The gaslight of the city squares lay behind them. They turned onto Peel Street. Shotgun houses and shrimp stands. The residences had their doors painted blue to keep out anything evil. The dry sand before them chirped in crickets. One or two shrimp stands were still open. You could smell the boil. Rich and red, sharp pepper cut into the air. Black men passed a wine bottle and dropped shrimp into their mouths. One laughed and busted a bottle against a brick foundation.

Alfbender led them off Peel Street and down across a vacant lot. Fallen chimneys. Milkweed and briers. Following Jess, Blake breathed in the aroma of the ambergris. When he was a boy Jess had told him how it was milked from the great whales of the sea, her eyes thrown open wide, so wonderfully surprised in the young and trembling excitement of new mothers who tell their first stories and see them light the long lashes of their children. To Blake, ambergris was the symbol of her mystery. At school when he was young and his pockets were cluttered with erasers and ice cream money, when the other boys smoked their cigarettes in the dirty stalls and kept their smell of smoke about them for the day, Blake, stepping quietly into the cloakroom, could always sense the ambergris of his mother's last kiss. In this way her presence was so unlike his father's: the clean quick soap of a man's shaving which went so fast away and left you alone and vulnerable to all the hurts of the world.

His father had been no mystery. Raised in the West, he was black-haired and blue-eyed. He left home at sixteen. He worked in the blue of Montana, then raced into the last days of vaudeville and a certain nearness to a kind of fame. No, Blake was sure fathers kept no secrets, especially in the fall evenings (very much like this one) when, returned from work, they began to dream of the first friendly burn of whiskey and, taking a glass, sat out in the wood-burning air holding you upon their knees, their eyes licorice-black by darkness in the stillness of the leafy air. Upon porches in the twilight they remembered past days and laughed in slim ribs growing whiskey warm and told you their way-wandering-west stories of hoboes and blue-knuckled fights. Fathers could not keep themselves down. They wove and rambled like a thicket, the stories and songs lighting up in them like fireflies among the brambles.

Mothers were not so easy to mark, even when you were a hand away. Some wore aprons and a clean face of plates and well-mended children. Others seemed worn like cloth and ground away their days behind cash registers and the threat of eviction. Most of them were quiet. Most meek and un-knowing of themselves.

Jess had nothing to do with aprons and meekness.

They crossed Abercorn Street and passed by its large

graveyard. For some reason, and though Blake thought he had bolted down the last fears about his father, the man's image rose again. He stopped and leaned against the cemetery fence. Blake had been able to deal with his father's passing because he had consigned him to peace and paradise. Well, perhaps not paradise, but at least painlessness. Now and again the childish thought of hell entered his mind.

Jess found him staring at the headstones.

"You know, sometimes I feel like he needed something here which we never gave him." He could feel his mother's eyes working the levels in him. "After years of games I think he finally just went down and we never knew it."

"Hush now."

"Nobody cared. Nobody listened. We just let him sink away into despair."

"He had many clever edges. He was vicious. Let him pass now."

"He never hurt anybody really."

"If you had the guts I would show you the scars."

"Don't lie about him. Don't do it."

"Laddie—"

"You let *them* wound him. *Your* brother. *Your* sister."

"Mr. Buckles, baby." She sighed and pulled him to her. "Lay your head here."

Blake felt the warmth of her breast against his face.

"What do you hear?"

"A heart."

"More."

"I just hear your heart!"

"When you father wished it—and he wished it often—he could smother my heart in his broad-handed wit like a wren. Still, I loved him. Pack him off now and be strong."

"You know, I think you love the wounds of this family."

Jess let him free. "And why did you really come home? Was school so difficult?"

"There's a ship." He stepped away. "I can get out into the world. I can do some good when I find my place."

"You plan to just sail away?"

"This family is a pillory to me." "Pillory" was his mother's word.

"Well, I do think we all fashion our own stocks. I have mine. And you—you turn over the days of your father's life one by one. Bruise by bruise and will not forget and bury and become a man. My, such a brave boy. Such a strapping lad. Afraid at nineteen to let your good ole daddy rot away to bones and a rack of teeth."

"Leave me alone."

"Poor baby. Why don't you try a few school remedies. Smoke a little pot ot shoot a little scag. At least have a couple of affairs. Whatever, Mr. Buckles, realize that Daddy has gone beddy-bye."

Blake slipped his hands over his ears. Jess pulled them away.

"Understand that Daddy is a sack of tripe and formalde-hyde and nothing can raise him up again."

Her voice broke then and Blake felt her arms around him. He could smell her bad teeth and the sweetness of the am-bergris and feel the wetness on her cheeks. He shivered.

"Quiet now," Jess said, holding him more tightly. "Forgive me, but you see you pushed Mother hard and she used the old balls shot. Daddy's—Daddy's alright. Look up at the stars. Go ahead. Look."

Blake saw them through the trees.

"See that one? See it? Maybe Daddy's up there. High and full of light. Not down here in his body, but in radiance and dancing and laughing and doing his best acts. A star in a star, Mr. Buckles. Prince of the hardwood stages. Best boy of the ringing light."

Just behind them Alfbender was speaking very rapidly.

"Alright—they're in the park and coming this way now."

Across the street, heading steadily for them, Blake saw the two red masks. Alfbender leapt ahead. Blake grabbed Jess's hand and pulled her along.

Raphael leaned against a tree and popped off his mask. He watched the three forms ahead of him. He grinned and lit up a Lucky Strike.

"*I think we should nab Jess and take her straight back to Cross. Now that's what I was told.*" *Thaggart was short, freckled, and out of breath.*

"*Naw,*" *Raphael said. He massaged the back of Thaggart's neck.* "*Cross took me aside and said just to watch them awhile. He said we might find out where Jess has been getting those illegal prescriptions. He said to follow her, and if nothing turns up to bring her home before too late.*" *Cross had really told them both to get her straight home. But Raphael was having fun. He moved beside a cannon in the center of the park. Around him the tall houses cast out party light. Their jasmined verandas held punch bowls and people. Raphael laid his head against the cannon's muzzle.* "*Boom,*" *he said.* "*I bet these things just went boom.*" *He blew a mouthful of smoke into the muzzle.*

"*Well, I don't know about you, but I got to work in the morning. I ain't going to have this thing drag on all night now.*"

"*How many folks you 'spect this thing blew up? A hundred? Maybe a thousand, huh?*"

"*What the hell are you saying now?*"

"*And where'd they all go to? The starless night? Ca-blam. Ca-blam-be-bam.*"

"*I don't like wearing these damn masks either,*" *Thaggart said.*

"*Come on now, Thag. It's fun.*"

"*Look here, they're way on down yonder. We're going to lose them standing here talking.*"

Raphael looked toward the river and the night. "I can smell them. Oh, Lordie, I can smell them and track them." His tooth slipped him a pain. He pulled out the old clove and stuck in a new one. He took a drag off his cigarette and felt happy. He felt like getting on all fours and howling and baring his teeth. Not now. No, no. Not yet.

Raphael extended his arms and made a noise like an airplane sawing through the dark.

After four or five blocks Alfbender stopped. They were all blowing hard, but took small breaths now and listened: the sound of traffic, a siren far away.

"Birddogs know the city pretty good," Alfbender said.

Jess was wiping sweat from her face and slapping it on her backside. "Brother . . ." She took a breath. "Brother is so good at inspiring these little events. He should have been a coach instead of a monster."

"Let's kick it for River Street," Alfbender said, starting up again.

"Nope. This old girl has placed and that's all she can do."

"We're going to take them on bare-handed?"

They stood now in a meaty-smelling alley. The right-hand side was made five blocks long by one building. Glazed windows went up into the night. Long gutters drained onto the pavement. Dead vines climbed the brick.

"I have to sit down," Jess said.

On the corner below the alleyway stood the Oyster House. Blue lights flashed in sequence: Oysters—Crabs—Bream.

To Blake the lights seemed blurred, the distance unsure. Running had probably brought up his fever again. He wrapped his forearm along his mother's waist. "We could rest in the Oyster House."

Alfbender swept at his hair. "If you want to get caught, that's a fine place to wait."

"Nobody wants to get caught, Alfbender," Jess said. "I need to sit down, that's all."

"Swell," Alfbender clipped. He went around the corner of the building and out of sight.

"We need him," Blake said.

"Tonight I trust him. I do. I know how he thinks and tonight he's okay," Jess said.

The restaurant smelled of sawdust and the piercing odor of shellfish. They sat down at a wooden counter. On the wall behind the counter hung decorative fishing nets, and centered between them and several rusting harpoons hung a large poster of Satan. Yellow eyes, a black tail and horns. He pointed a finger toward the counter. TEXAS "HOT" TABASCO SAUCE was printed beneath the cloven feet.

A rangy, yellow-skinned waitress marched out of the kitchen. A cigarette drooped from her lips as she took beers to three or four men down the bar.

"Yep," she said to Blake.

"Oh, just a couple iced teas," he said.

Jess placed her fingertips to Blake's temples. "You're hot. Red as a beet."

"Just a virus."

"You're sure?"

The waitress clacked the tea down. Blake laid out fifty cents.

His throat was sore again. The iced tea made it hurt. He wondered how he had gotten down with mono. He had only necked a little bit at school. He wasn't very good at all that stuff.

The screen door behind and to the left of the counter opened. A black man entered pulling a wooden wagon behind him. He wore a train cap with a small red feather stuck in its side. He was bituminous black, the membranes of his eyes nearly blue. Blake nudged his mother. She looked up

39

but did not smile as the black man pulled his wagon into the kitchen.

In a moment the man returned and sat down two stools from Blake.

"Doing just fine, how are you?" Blake said.

Teetat's head never turned, but his eyes cut a slow arc to Blake.

"You hungry?" Teetat asked in a raw voice.

Blake sat beside him, grabbed his shoulders. "I've missed you, Teetat. I even wrote a paper about you at school. What you been doing since you left us?" Teetat smelled of crab and sulfur mud.

"Been down in the marsh." He kept his eyes low. "I haul in some good crab."

Jess finished her tea, then went to the ladies' room.

"Your mama never liked me a whole lot," Teetat said.

"She's just nervous."

"You should be, too." Teetat's black fingers stroked his sideburns.

"You think the family's crazy. I know. I just came to get Mother out of here, then I'm off."

Teetat turned and stuck two fingers beneath Blake's belt. The black face was cold. "They're not crazy. Crazy means you can't do for yourself, and they do just fine. You get yourself away, boy. You can't see them like I can."

Jess banged the toilet door and approached noisily. "Well, Teetat, how are you?"

"Been setting traps in the shallows and taking my catch."

"And?"

"It's cold down there. But I like the marsh, and the hardshells sell. It's all I know."

"You always have the best blue crabs in town." Jess motioned Blake up.

Blake looked at Teetat, then went to the door.

"Some things you don't want to catch. They are too delicate. They just die and rot in the traps. You know?" Teetat turned his face to her.

Jess opened the door and directed Blake out to the street.

"He's a dangerous nigger," Jess said, not softly.

"You have to know him. He's really kind of gentle," said Blake.

"Well, I *do* know that we have to catch the ferry to get to my place so I can see what I need from there."

"I know a shortcut." Blake took her hand and stepped off the curb.

He decided to zigzag his way toward the river. Not follow any one street. He worried about Alfbender. He should have appeared by now. Had Cross paid him off? But Jess seemed sure of him and she knew him best.

He glanced at Jess. She was moving well and seemed content. She seemed happy on the march. Blake realized now that at these times of familial war he felt very even about her. Her face seemed lovely and bold in the passing lights. The suffering that had filtered through her eyes and settled beneath them lent her a separate beauty. In this movement away from something pursuing them, he reached a longed-for completeness with her as if through the simple act of aiding one another again he had come upon a sense of his boyhood when he was so magically part of her, his will indistinguishable from her own. By her smiles and words, which he did not understand then, nor wish to understand, by the motion of her delicate neck and hands, by the honey-eyed texture of her laughter, he was much more than alive as a boy—he was pure and essential as the breath of her wondrous life.

Ahead of them two or three spider monkeys were shrieking in the palmettos. Two figures were standing very quietly before a fountain.

"A little chatter under the starlight," Jess said.

"Let's move around these two people," Blake said carefully.

"No red."

"Masks come off. Let's cut around."

One of the fingers began waving at them.

"Something's not right here," Jess said, going toward the fountain.

Blake followed her, watching the two people cautiously.

The flagstone in front of the fountain was covered by bits of palm and excrement, and the monkeys were screaming louder now.

"I have nothing against monkey see, but monkey do is a bit much," Jess said, hoisting her foot up and scraping her shoe against the fountain's circular wall.

A woman thin and brown as pie crust stared at the fountain, one large finger pressed against the side of her nose. She waved Blake closer, turned her full scowling face toward the trees, and reached up and snapped off her hearing aid.

"Somebody's gone nuts," her husband said, looking at the base of the fountain.

"There's no doubt. Not a little bit," Blake said, trying to take his eyes off the large melting ice cream cone in the man's hand. He looked at the fountain but saw nothing.

"Oh, yeah. The fellow doing this kind of thing's gone whistling way on down the tracks."

Blake searched the pool. It seemed empty and still.

"Hell, I'd go on in there, but they got things, I hear—diseases—and I'd just as soon let the city come and get it." He flashed a thin smile. His glasses flicked a little streetlight.

Blake leaned over the wall of the fountain. The monkeys began screaming and racing up and down scraping bark. Then, on the fountain's center column, he made out an object—hanging.

"If you had to call it I'd say he was some kind of psycho doing things like this. Hell, there's not a nickel's sense in it."

"Hey!" Blake said and pointed.

Jess got beside him.

He could see it now. A monkey tied about the upper base. The eyes were wide and even seemed to be full of light. The long body and arms were moving loosely in the streams of water. Blake pulled off his shoes and waded into the pool. Warm water. Sludge beneath his feet.

Coming closer, he hoped that the animal was merely unconscious. Hesitantly he reached out a hand for the chest. The fur felt cold. He could sense no breathing. He pulled back, looking at the tight wire which was now distending the belly. The entire chest cavity had been slashed open.

The old lady still had her finger against her nose. Her husband was addressing himself to the chocolate sleeve of his coat. "I'll get a cop and he'll get a nigger. We'll manage to get this place clean again. Damn. It's dead beasts or pickaninnies pissing in it or something. But we'll get her cleaner'n Job's cash box." They began walking toward a phone booth. He turned back to Blake. "Damn well better peroxide that finger, buddy. They say they got diseases, you know?"

Blake stepped out of the pool. Put on his shoes. He slowly rubbed his hands together, trying to keep composed, searching out lights in the distance.

"Pretty bad, I guess," Jess said.

Blake kept silent.

"Tales have been going around."

"It's been gutted."

Jess glanced at the corpse. "We should get it down now."

"They went for the cops."

She drew her arms about herself. "Could I—could I borrow one of your yellows?"

Even now the question went coldly into Blake. "It's always a step down for you."

"Good name, downers." She tried to smile.

Blake gave her a couple and put his arm around her and

43

started walking north toward the river again. Jess began to turn, but he kept her straight. "It's nothing to do with us," he said. "I'm hungry. Let's eat something on the ferry."

They made their way down to the lower end of River Street for the ferry. At the harbor the sea was pulling the tidal pools back into itself, and the white moon smoothly sifted down the channels of water, silver and cutting along the clean ribbed sand. On one of the squares behind them a church bell tolled ten o'clock.

The ferry waited at the docks for the half-hour crossing. Electric light shone from her deck, and the linen of the dining tables was starched and unstirring in the breeze. Stew and coffee simmered on a gas stove behind the tables, and in the darkness about the stern rows of bananas and pomegranates bobbed slowly from the harbor's current.

They paid a dollar and came aboard and sat down at one of the tables.

A noisy dredger worked the center of the harbor. Red and green lights flashed on its rusting flanks. A spotlight from the operator's platform lit up a twenty-foot area. Yellow water and oil slicks. The iron jaws now were being hauled up to the top of the crane. Blake could not see them, but the engine was growling and he knew they were there. The engine shifted to a soft clacking. There was a whistling sound. The jaws struck down through the surface and went for the bottom. In the spotlight the iron mug came up draining black sand and seaweed and sewage. The crane heavily swiveled left and emptied debris into the sled.

The air stank. The dredger growled again. Iron worked the night.

Blake surveyed the docks.

"Something?" Jess said.

"Thought I saw a little red glowing out there."

"Hoboes doing a little squeeze," she said in a comforting voice.

44

A barefoot waiter shuffled up, and they ordered the special.

The waiter mumbled the order to himself in slow Gullah and went back to the galley.

"There's something I've wondered about since I was a kid. Where do animals go when they die? You never see dead ones, unless they've been killed. Maybe they just—go on."

"There *are* monsters, aren't there, Buckles?" Jess said, gazing back at the luminescent squares of the city.

"I don't know. I think there may be."

"How marvelous. What handiwork."

"Some need, somewhere."

Jess paused and tugged at her ear. "You know, those few times when your father and Alfbender put me in the hospital, they were so clever about it. So boyish. Oh, it hurt—the idea that I had been outthought, outfought, and bushwacked again. But there was such fun."

Blake kept his eyes still.

"Now, Cross—he always did things to hurt. Always sent bums to slap on the bracelets and only stood close enough to watch or smell. Your uncle has the most profound nose."

The fresh melon was set down before them. The wedges were cool and green and the juice sparkled and began to fill the white plate. The stew was ladled out of a black pot and the oysters and crabmeat made little room for the dark sauce of Bristol sherry and cream.

Blake took a spoonful of soup. The taste became more than just the stew. It was this place, this time—it was home and the night light of Port Sound. He watched Jess and wondered why he had never before noticed the beauty of her hands. The resolve with which they worked and the elegance of her fingers.

"You look uptown tonight," Blake said.

She raised her eyes a little.

"People don't say those things much. Sons don't. So I thought . . . well, I thought I'd say it."

Jess touched his hand.

"When you get past sixteen or so, you begin to see things in mothers that are—more than you first thought," Blake said.

Jess was wiping the melon from her hands and taking Blake carefully word by word, and the second and third motions behind the words. "We see things, too. We feel new and good dimensions. Your boat trip sounds good to me. When do you leave?"

Her words came down honest. Blake felt cheered. "I don't know yet. I haven't even gotten my seaman's papers yet. I'm sure it's not that hard to get on a boat. I'd love to go down through the Caribbean."

"You'll learn so many things."

"Are you really for it?"

"Damn right."

"I need you to say that. When you say that, I get stronger."

"You're my boy. You're strong."

"No, I'm not. I blush. I still turn red over the silliest things."

"Well, that will clear up. Sailors are rough. The sea is rough. You'll learn to cuss and you'll be alright."

"I just have this dream of doing something worthwhile out there. Something adventurous and good."

"Like what?"

"Oh, I don't know for sure. Sometimes I think of myself in a dusty village. Twilight. Lightning crackling in the air. Jungle all around. And all these people suddenly come to my hut. Cut and wounded. There's been an explosion. A volcano or something. I sew up their wounds. I happen to have some penicillin with me, and I stitch up their cuts and make them all well. They cry. I cry. Something like that. Something good and way off in a jungle. I even audited a nursing course at school. Stitches aren't so hard to do."

Jess laughed gently and squeezed his forearm and worked her fingers into the tendon. Her face was plain strength, her eyes green and calm.

She felt proud of him, Blake knew. This was the sweet face of pride.

"You used to practice on your teddy bear. Bet you don't remember that?"

"Sewing him up?"

"You worked on him all day long sometimes. Oh, Merthiolate and bandages and silver thread."

"I cut him first, though. I took a razor and slashed him right open."

"Like a surgeon. Like a doctor."

"I got joy out of cutting the bear. I did. I remember that now." Blake felt dark and worried. He thought of the gutted monkey.

"But you also got joy out of fixing him back again. Mending him. Remember that now. Don't be so harsh with yourself."

"I suppose," Blake said, returning.

"Besides, the sea will make you new. Wash you clean and keep you fit."

Blake felt her changing the subject. He needed it.

"You'll go into port. Have a drink. See all kinds of sights. Dance with those Latin girls. They will adore you, Buckles."

"Well, maybe. Nothing like that's worked out so far."

"It will. You just need some time."

Jess finished up her stew.

The ferry was nearing the other dock.

"You haven't seen my new apartment, have you?" Jess asked.

"The old roundhouse?"

"So many bricks. Two square miles of brick walls and

47

canals and warehouses. Now and again I take a cue from Cross and pretend that I am high priestess of it all. There, I am Coatlicue sitting among the ruins of my dreams."

Blake changed his accent to something sounding foreign and forced his eyes to slits. "You offered oblations to the great god Huitzilopochtli, the Blue Hummingbird?"

"And to Quetzalcoatl, magnificent Lord of Cactus Rock!"

"Ah, the old gods live and their need for blood is great."

Jess took on a more serious face. A salt breeze blew her skirt, ruffled her blouse. She turned her face toward the sky.

The pink rings of her neck. The small cluster of veins under her chin.

"Stars are wicked things, Buckles."

"I think they're pretty nice."

"You listen to me. They are as cold as a cabbage heart. They conspire. They plot. Surrounded by the dark it is their nature, their relief to seek out amusement and mischief. One family. Bright drones and dangerous on account of it. Do you see what I'm saying?"

A scene. Beautiful words. Blake understood. She'd been talking too straight too long. "Of course," he said.

The ferry bumped against the dock.

The waiter soughed barefoot across the deck. He threw out a line and tied them up. Blake left money on the table.

As the ferry pulled back across the river, they climbed wooden stairs and stood on a small dune of sand.

"When do you get the telegram?" Blake asked.

"There's a station at the roundhouse. Eleven-thirty, the agent said."

"You think Alfbender has been bought yet?"

"He'll appear. He was the first one to push me for the play."

"You really want this part?"

"It's a tough one. I always did the funny parts here. This is real. I can feel it."

48

"But you're going up there for more than the play, right? To start something. To get out on your own."

"Cross and Millis I love but never needed. Only your father kept me here. Now, I'm ready for big bands and fancy lights."

"Cross worries me."

"A little power play at the end. My last fun with little brother." She became quiet. "Still, we shouldn't let Birddogs get too close. Sometimes they *do* mangle and retrieve."

They began walking down Parnell Street toward the railway yards.

In the moonlight and the steam pushing away from palmettos and green sedge, the buildings of the roundhouse seemed to Blake to be in motion: a slight, almost courtly weaving toward the nearby inlets and then the land. For years now the walls had been going down beneath their hard slate roofs and iron beams through a melody of disunions, mortar and wood tumbling silently into the black dirt of the shops. Jess stepped through the plank fence and Blake followed her across the long prairie of the yard. Easing into the first tall shop, he became aware of space as solemn and encompassing as the broad running planes of cathedrals. There was here a kind of thin light from wall to ceiling, a spindling of lassitude and emptiness weaving above the ferns that had pried into the bricks of the walls and the weeds, some as tall as masts, which sought out the starlight through the fragile and wind-tinkling glass of the roof. And as Jess moved quickly ahead along a walk of boards, Blake became aware, too, of the silence here which stood watch over discarded and grand wheels of locomotives and long-jawed union rods and the spines of boxcars. It was a quietness at once hard and empty as the long reaches of this building, but verdant too, examining, preciously filled with life sprung from the rotting floors or the tendrils of nearby inlets holding here minnows and tiny crabs.

Jess stopped.

"What's the rent?" Blake quipped.

"I'm known as a squatter. Dreadfully common and rather chic."

"I don't see how you could stay in this place."

She pointed at a small door just ahead of him. "I keep the linen in there. Go in two rooms deep and say hello to Filigree."

Blake had first met Filigree while visiting Jess in the State Hospital. The old man had been a set designer, a high-school art teacher. He was loony now.

"I'm going to the new spur for the telegram."

She waved a mock salute and went down a flight of stairs. Blake steadied himself for Filigree.

The first room had a sink, one burning lamp, sofa, and chairs. Blake looked into the second. Above the center of the bed hung an enormous bronze telescope. Along the sides of the main cylinder flashed the heads of bolts; just below them, peaks of black metal and the silver faces of mirrors jutted out; and above the mirrors stood small cups of steel that looked like urns, while beside these lay even smaller doors— some finely etched and having brass handles—apparently leading into the works of the machine, which appeared to be magically suspended from a completely solid and opaque ceiling.

Making a little noise so as not to startle the old man, Blake moved around the headboard toward the foot of the bed.

Filigree lay at the very end of the telescope's eyepiece, the cup only two inches from his socket and his white hair, which fell down over his shoulders and onto a mound of soiled pillows.

"I already paid for the damn condoms," the old man screeched.

"Wrong fellow," Blake said.

"I don't like all those funny colors, anyway."

"Me either."

"Drop your pants, bucko," Filigree said.

Blake winced a little.

"I know you," Filigree said, raising up on one elbow. A necklace of wooden crosses clinked around his neck. "I know them green eyes and all that mouth."

"I always wanted to look more like my father."

"That sonofabitch! That papist!"

"Acquainted with him?"

"I knew the whole sleazy crowd. Where's your ma?"

"Looking for a telegram."

"Drop your pants and let's have a little look at the moon!"

Blake went over and felt the telescope. The bronze gave in like paper. He looked more closely. It *was* paper.

"How's it look up there?" he asked, studying the piece of work.

"The angels are coming," Filigree said. "A small party. A point of light now. Second quadrant at thirty-six north. I jack off as many times a week as I can now since I first saw the blue of their eyes out there."

"Why would they come here?" Blake asked quietly.

"To work. To do for us."

"Maybe they're adventurers."

"They laugh. They open their silver mouths and smile."

"You believe in them, though. I mean—enough to touch one."

"They are real."

"I wish they were. I wish something that good was real."

"A needle's eye of brightness."

"When I was little I prayed so hard to see one. Just one. When I was little. But he never came."

"The blue of their eyes in the dark."

"Yeah, we could all use angels."

"The angels are coming and they are bright with keys."

"Maybe that's all we need, just a few good keys. Just a way to get in and out."

"You really going to let her go if she gets that part?"

"She needs to be free."

"She needs you. She should be bound in love. Yep, thank you, doctor, only the damned are free."

"Listen. I go on my own and that's her style too."

"You think Cross—you think Mr. Humpty Dumpty's going to let her go?"

"It's his last game with her."

"Two men. Red masks and they are looking to keep her here. One of them's trouble. One of them's crazier than me."

"When?"

"A few minutes ago."

"What did they want?"

"Plums and rice pudding."

Blake went for the door.

"Have you ever seen the way bums move when they're packing the works? Oh so soft. Like kids carrying dandelions. They moved like that. They got needles and the sleep on them."

"Cross can't do that. He's got no reason this time."

Filigree laughed and the crosses rattled around his neck. "Humpty Dumpty will splatter apart if your mother leaves. I taught him design in school. I saw all the lines go crooked in him away back."

Blake again moved for the door.

"I sent them on a little chase. Threw them off a while."

"Somebody's going to have to take his teeth out one of these days," Blake said.

"In school Millis and Cross always held right on to her. Never could leave her. And if you pulled them apart, Millis cried and Cross would cut himself with his pocketknife or jab a pencil into his hand. When she was in the hospital with me, when they had us in the wards, she'd get out of bed late at night and tend to us that was tied down and couldn't pee or scratch. The love in her is something and you don't quite see it, do you?"

"I can see."

"Millis and Cross tried to eat her up at the old home place and *you* let them."

"No," Blake said.

"You left her."

"It's not my place."

"The angels will love her."

"You're nuts."

"I'm saved."

"Yeah."

"My telescope sees the angels."

Suddenly Blake clenched his hands around the old man's throat. "All those times she prayed. All those sober, clear nights she cried, 'Don't let me end up in that place again.' But were the angels dispatched? The loveliest of us all, and time after time she was tossed back into the State Hospital. You did it, Filigree! Making up stories about angels. There are no angels! I'd like to stretch your neck. I'd like—"

Blake had the old man's neck in his hands, twisting the face purple, when he heard her calling his name and felt himself being pulled away.

Filigree began throwing up. Jess quickly knelt by the bed, her hands supporting Filigree's head. Blake backed away.

Jess held the old man until his coughing subsided into a gray wheeze and a little whisper: "I got the syph. I got the syph. Way down inside me I got the syph."

Looking at Blake in a short, hard way, Jess opened a box beside the bed. "Come here," she said. She placed a spoon in his hand, reached back into the box, pinched a little white powder, and sifted it into the spoon, adding a drop of water. She struck a match and held it beneath the spoon and stirred, carefully keeping her eyes off Blake.

Filigree was still singing, his white hair scattered over his face. "Black bean soup. I'm black bean soup. Rotting through and through. Rotting . . ."

Jess filled the syringe and pumped a vein and slid the needle in.

"Whee! Oh whee!" the old man squealed. His face was swelling with blood.

For a while she kept close to him. She pulled a sheet to his neck and brushed back his hair. She tied the strands into a ponytail and bound them with a small tortoise-shell clamp and kissed him on his watery eyes.

The stars were clear and sharp. Blake sat down beside Jess on the stone wall which formed the pit for the spindle. Here the locomotives had been spun into the shops. The lanky spindle still sat waiting above brackish pools and layers of mosquitoes whining by the damp stones.

"You get tough on old men, huh?" Jess said.

"He lied."

"You were going to break his neck for that?"

"He was lying, Mama. He had been telling you something that wasn't so. False hope."

"Where's this bad edge coming from? All this violence."

"It's family stuff."

"We never struck people."

"Not with fists."

"No. If there was some violence, we kept it among ourselves."

"I just thought he was hurting you. Making you believe in something other than me or yourself."

"Well, how does it feel to let the beast have your hands?"

"It does allow you to feel."

"I don't think so."

"I just see that now in myself. To make something hurt, to cause pain fills up some holes."

"You didn't get that from me."

"I used to crucify birds, you know."

"A little boy's hobby."

"When their eyes twisted fast and then went still, I felt

54

sad. And when I felt sad, guilty—I could pray and then feel better."

"So Buckles is looking for something to plug the holes."

"No. I've got that now. I know what I want to do."

"What? Save the world?"

"I want to save you. I want to get you away from this family." He paused. "Filigree says Birddogs were here."

"I was told at the telegraph."

"Has it come yet?"

"Probably a little tie-up. Lots of gals honking for the part."

"Got the sleep on them, the old man said. Works and the big sleep."

"How does he know?"

"Something about the way they were walking."

Jess was working her thumb through her fingers.

"You know, once I thought I knew all the currents of this family. Where to cut in close and where by God to go for the groundswells and stay clear of the rest. Maybe it's not a game for Cross. If those bums really do have the needle on them again, maybe Cross has had a little breakdown. There's something not right about all this."

"Sometimes I'd like to get heavy on Cross because of this meanness he's got in him. But I have problems with that. I feel—and it is feeling rather than thinking—I feel like Cross is good essentially. Like all of them two steps down are good. They don't really intend to hurt us."

Jess sighed a little, bundled up her skirt between her legs. She picked at some cool tiger lilies around the wall. "But they do damage. Knowing or unknowing. Whether or not their veins are flowing with milk and honey. They do pin you. They do pry loose every last stone." She began braiding a flower around Blake's wrist. "Did you know the last time I was taken off to the hatchery that Cross—having bribed Alfbender with two silver flutes and boxes of Bavarian chocolates—did you know that he sent flowers every day and wrote me poems and drew me the most precious little water-colors?"

"You're kidding?"

"And when the nurses pasted on the wires and strapped me down and told me not to worry while they headed nimbly-timbly for their rubber mats—even at that point I could not set one black marble against him."

"This last time I should have fought. I was frightened. Cross moves so fast. I didn't know how to stop him."

"Cross always prided himself on his fastness. His ability to rattle off mortality tables and Aztec gods."

"Why didn't you set a few traps for him?"

"Occasionally I am able to snip his roots clean as a ribbon. My plans are always so ponderous, so slow. I did take him once when he was very young and not so damned quick. He was nineteen and in love. Oh, how his little black heart beat like a beetle. He had recently contracted hepatitis from some late-night rudeness conducted in the lower part of town, or so I surmised. At any rate, he was supposed to mend his liver and stay in bed for a while. His girl friend was my great confidante. She did not care for Cross's heart so much as she did for his back. He was a complement to her small dairy. Loading and unloading, busy as a cub in a honey tree. I was able to map the plan out well. One day I rushed into his room and announced silly-eyed with happiness how Olivia had just confessed to me that she loved him godlessly, but that she could not leave her husband nor could she show Cross any more real affection, which grieved her to the grain of her soul. (Olivia knew nothing of my plan.) I let this notion molder in him a while. He developed more pain and a little fever, I believe. Then I set the cheese on the trigger. I came to him one evening and confided, drooping my face, wrin-kling my eyes, that her business was about to fold. Her hus-band was drunk and not helping her. Cows were drying up like mud puddles. Calves were sucking wind. For the next two weeks he worked sixteen-hour days. At night I read him little notes saying how much she loved him, though neither of them must show it. His heart was breaking. His liver was bursting. He was flushed pink and cheerful as a cherry at the barns in the day and lay green as grapes in his bed at night. Finally he began to look unpleasantly pregnant and one day fainted in a pained lump of liver and bile at the creamer. In the hospital, when they thought he lay in his last flicker, I whispered deliciously into his ear that the whole time she was only teasing him, joking. I had hoped this last little pebble of despair would scuttle him down—of course it did not."

Blake was reading her face carefully. "A pretty hateful plan."

"Bitter, but adroit."

"But you liked it. It was fun?"

"I rolled over it like a bitch on a bone."

"You think Cross remembers?"

"He quakes at cream to this very day. Beating your brother badly is a natural high. It is truly redemptive."

Blake nudged her. "How much of all that happened?"

Jess primped at the flowers about Blake's wrist. "Oh . . . it was the plan."

"Did it happen?"

She made a little humming noise. "Well . . . I suppose not. But I did think of doing it, you see. I *could* be more than a victim. I could be sinister, too."

Blake twirled the stems about his wrist. The bracelet came undone. He thought that maybe families were no different than the outside: victims and those who did them in. He wondered if somewhere in the sleeping genes of his mother there had been passed to him a form of her own passivity.

Something gave way in the dark.

They kept still. Blake raised his head. From behind him came another noise.

"Lie down," he whispered to Jess.

Toward the south yard beside the lighted warehouses, he saw two men moving. They no longer wore the masks. But they were Birddogs. Blake could sense them. He wondered if Cross was simply trying to frighten Jess, threatening her, but he feared Filigree's perceptions and that maybe they did carry the works on them and Cross in desperation had actually decided to put her back into the asylum.

The two figures waited in the shadows, then disappeared out a side gate.

"We have to get out of here," Blake said.

"I need to get back to the wire office."

"It's just fine bait there."

"Calm down."

"Let Alfbender get the telegram if he's still working with us."

Jess gave a little whistle and tucked at her hair and tapped her toes in getting up. "It seems that I have never progressed beyond basic training in this family. Oh well, let's see. We'll break behind enemy lines and hide out. Ho, ho. We'll sneak into a place not even Cross could stake out—the Wheeler Street Halloween Fair."

Blake had never missed the fair as a boy. He loved the trumpeters and the fiestalike feeling. Wheeler Street was the place to hide.

They slipped out of the train yard and moved down a side lane. About them renovated railroad houses brimmed full of light. Most of them stood out as angular and having three floors and balconies leafy with plants. To the side of the houses stairs spindled down to plank-wall gardens. A block farther down the renovation stopped and the black part of town, the slums, began.

Badly paved streets and long rows of airless, bleached-board hovels, the rusting tin of their roofs holding city heat and despair. The front yards of the houses were grassless, but

by the streetlights you could see that the dirt had been carefully raked. A blue ceramic Madonna stood in one patch of
earth, while before another dwelling tomato plants grew
from cans painted blue and brown, yellow and white. This
part of town had no oaks. No moss. No trees at all. Just
sandy porches and grim steps and raked city earth with the
heat of the day still there. On the corner, even though the air
was still warm enough to make you sweat, a fire burned in an
ashcan. Two or three old colored men sat on peach crates
beside the fire, hats cocked over their eyes. When Blake said
hello, they grinned and looked away.

They made their way farther down. Around two corners
and to the right, a good two miles from the downtown
squares, lay Wheeler Street.

A mud road. Ragged row houses on either side and these
painted the softest of colors: pink and violet, gray and rose.
Sagging lines of light bulbs ran alongside the road and
brought several hundred blacks into high relief. Though few
wore costumes or masks, most of them were dressed in bril-
liantly colored suits and dresses. The men strode about in
purples, greens, and lion-yellow broadcloth, on their heads
wearing hats made of crushed velvet or gangsterlike felt.
Their shoes were alligator hide and gold buckles. Standing
mostly apart from the men, the women had rouged cheeks,
flaky lipstick, and mascara. A study in extremes, they
primped on porch steps, giving inviting smiles and salty
winks, or disregarded the entire affair, scowling in feigned
boredom.

Most of the crowd gathered near the center of the street
before the Only Globe Ball Room. Blake remembered when
the nightclub had opened some ten years ago there had been
a furor. But the place had finally been accepted because it
was viewed as a circus: a place to sip gin and offer catcalls as
the patrons entered and left the club.

The Only Globe had six pillars and an overhanging portico. The pillars were wooden and, like the rest of the building, needed paint. The upper-floor windows had been smashed out. Underwear and rags had been crammed into the smaller holes. Fluffy pigeon nests and clumps of city weeds grew out of the gutters, but when tuxedoed waiters eased out onto the porch for a smoke and mulatto women were visible dancing behind the old glass, the place became a nighttime palace.

Sliding out of the boxwoods, munching a corndog, Alfbender stepped up toward Blake and Jess.

"And where the hell have you been?" Jess asked, clasping her hands behind her back and spreading her feet.

"I saw you leave from Filigree's. I been asking questions about these Birddogs. Some of the answers I got ain't too comforting."

Blake studied the lawyer's sly face. "You didn't go see Cross, did you, Alf? You didn't make a deal to go against us?"

Alfbender hooked a lock of hair behind one ear and took a bite of his corndog. He cinched a skinny thumb into his belt and sighed. "Nope."

Maybe you just lived with your lawyer's weasel eyes. "What did you find out?" Blake asked.

"One of those Birddog's is a crazy. Been in the nut house."

"Ah, a kindred spirit," Jess said.

"I don't think so," Alfbender said. "They found a dog cut up by the tracks. I'm worried. I'm concerned about a lot of things tonight. You two can stay here. It's okay for a while. I'll stand out front where I can watch some." He stuck the butt of his corndog into one of his enormous pockets and glided into the crowd.

Blake looked beyond the lights of the street. "You wonder what's going on once in a while."

"Alfbender's spooked."

"I know there are some bad things out there. But that

doesn't mean you give up, right? You don't go run and hide."

"Don't worry about all that. We're in the light and okay," Jess said smiling, and a small purple bar-room scar over her left cheek dimpled. She slid a hand into his back pocket. "Now I think we need a trip to the fun houses. Come on."

To the left of the Only Globe stood three busy sausage-biscuit huts. The crab soufflé stand had a rowdy double line, and the smell of green peppers and hot sausage and spiced crabmeat filled the air. Ahead of them a trumpet contest was starting up. Mostly old men in white shirts and ratted suspenders, bow ties and creased trousers.

The fun houses served as very ordinary vegetable stalls most of the year. But tonight they had been made into places of magic. In one fun house you could finally become whatever you had always wished to be by just selecting a costume and having your picture taken. In another you could hunt cardboard beasts with an air gun. One place drew Blake's attention. A house made of old windows. On the inside, snow sat in the corners of the panes. The floor seemed two feet deep in the stuff. Blake came closer. Snow?

Jess raced through the door and kicked off her shoes in the middle of a drift. Blake could actually see her breath. She laughed and waved him forward.

Blake went to the door. In the artificial coolness Jess seemed suddenly renewed, weariness lost from her face. She laughed and kicked at the snow. She spun around, color rising in her cheeks.

Blake wiped his eyes. Fever, he thought.

"Surf's up!" Jess yelled.

"Is it—real?"

"Yes. Oh yes, sweetheart!"

Unaccountably, Blake found himself backing away. Jess reached through the door, began tugging him in. Blake resisted, then felt a sting at his ankle and sprawled into the soft wetness. He let out a little gasp of air. He ran his hand

61

around him: tiny pieces of paper. He lifted up a palmful and let the flakes drift down on his face.

"This wasn't here last year," Jess said. She scooted down into the drift.

"You said it was real snow."

"It seemed real."

"But you knew that it wasn't." He looked up and saw a large air conditioner laboring in the corner.

"I didn't examine it. Look, they made it to be snow. They wanted it to be snow. So . . ." She threw a handful of flakes at him and started burying herself.

Blake let it go. He let it go and laughed and piled handfuls on top of her.

"More, more," she yelled, disappearing beneath the finely cut paper.

Blake was scooping the flakes over her.

"Shut your eyes. Close them tight until I say."

He closed his eyes and felt silly.

"Open now," she mumbled.

When Blake looked where she had been he saw only a white ridge. Searching more carefully he saw the sharp outline of her nose jutting out of the whiteness. He reached over and pinched it.

"Time out. You found me. Time out," Jess squealed.

Blake laughed.

There had been other light moments but they had always been long ago when there seemed to be no real progression in the days and acts were not known as the precedents to consequences. In those days time *was* only a word in a game. A word meaning that you were safe from your cap-gun hunters. "Time!" and you were safe and untouchable.

"Buckles! Listen up now. Tell me who I am." Jess cleared most of the snow away from her. "Name where this comes from . . . 'Bravely beneath the dark waters swam he. Beneath the grim currents of Charmion toward the twice-adorned towers of Marmilaya ... ' "

"I don't know."

" 'His golden knife and bow readied he while the breath taken from the pure leaves of Almidon slowly passed away ... ' "

"John Carter of Mars!"

" 'And as his soft lips and raven hair rose from the tarn, little did he know the arch villain waited above him in the night. The hunter in the dark.' " Jess was crouched and making faces like a villain.

"It's me. I made it up just now. It just came right out of me. It's good, isn't it? Maybe I could really be something one day."

Blake clapped his hands and rolled into the snow. Jess reached over and kissed his stomach.

They sat quietly, their backs against the glass.

"I think Daddy would have liked this place," Blake said.

"Loved it."

"Sometimes when I dream about him he doesn't seem to know that he's dead. I say, 'Daddy, you're supposed to be dead,' and he just smiles and says all that was a trick. 'It wasn't me in the box,' he says."

"You never beat him. He died too young. It's a shame you never knocked him to the floor one way or another. You have to deck your father to be rid of him. You have to defeat your family and earn your freedom."

Blake had never noticed this kind of strength in her before. This real part of her must have always been behind her joking face and warm hair and all the acts that mothers perform for their children. You could not see mothers clearly while you were young, perhaps because they waded in the full shadow of your father. Now lying beside her, Blake was almost startled to think of her as having life that was not an imitation of his father's, but a motion and sentience that was awesome in its own right. And Blake realized too that in a way which diminished his own strength he had begun to adore his father since his death, wiping away the bad parts of him and piling high in his memory the gentle man, the soft-spoken solver of problems and full-evening storyteller who mischievously slipped him bright-eyed quarters and talked man talk to him over black coffee on very special five o'clock mornings when the night lingered on. But perhaps to be still was best. Just let the man rise and fall, come and go in his mind the way the day would have him. Sometimes fabled and proud as the stars, at other times strange and troublesome as the manner of his passing.

"Maybe Daddy *did* do some real good in his lifetime," Blake said.

"What about me? I've accomplished a few things."

"You never say anything about yourself though."

"All that humble shuffling behind morning cereal."

"But, see, I knew him. He opened himself up to me."

"Of course I didn't. I was secretive and perverse."

"He just talked to me a lot about himself."

"I burbled?"

"There were bad times, I know that. But always to me he was entirely open, completely free."

"Never have I met in all of my life a man, your father, so totally, inextricably, and masochistically bound to himself, this family, and his spastic colon."

"Was he a good lover?" Blake wanted the scene now.

"He was persistent."

"But he knew his stuff."

"I had several affairs with him in the twenty years of our marriage."

"I *know* he was good."

"Is that what they call a shocking confession?"

"I listened sometimes."

"Sometimes we listened to you listening."

"You were loud."

"We were athletic."

"It frightened me sometimes and I prayed that Daddy would stop."

"Well, let it never be said that some prayers are not answered—repeatedly."

"Okay, okay. Why don't you tell me a secret about yourself then? He told me plenty about himself."

"I used to hang upside down in the shower and smoke dope."

"You see? You close me off. You camouflage yourself."

Jess put a hand over one of her eyes. "One parent's burdens are enough."

"Tell me anything. Something you wanted to be. Something you wanted to do."

Jess blew a few flakes into the air. "Okay. Alright. When I was very young, I wanted to bake the sweetest rolls and stitch clothes fit for princes and have a will as pure and bright as a nun's needle."

Blake smiled. "Thanks." He nudged his head against hers. "But—your cakes always fell, Mama."

"My breasts, I fear, are following suit."

"My patches were the lousiest ones at school."

"In your seesaw years my thumbs could turn the seas incarnadine."

"Still, you are beautiful."

"Oh, yes."

"Men still give you the eye. I've seen them looking."

"Looking ain't loving."

"I love you."

Jess stroked his face. "Sons stop loving their mothers just after toilet training. Something to do with acquiring privacy, I think."

"I love you," Blake said again quietly.

"You have a need to see me. To smell me. To—touch now

and again, I think. But love lives as only a very young creature. It dies brightly and wet-eyed, in thistle and down."

Blake felt himself part and open painfully. "You know I
heard this same kind of rhetoric between you and Daddy."

"Well then, learn a lesson. We do not love our families.
We are bound to them. You cannot love what chains you.
We are charged through DNA to cough like them, laugh like
them, and even twitch like them. We are by our families
doomed to only two new steps: the first and the last, both
made incoherently. The rest is a hard and heckling bondage."

Suddenly a black man stepped into the fun house. "You
got a friend wears a red bow, ma'am?"

"Alfbender," Jess said.

"He was standing by the street. Two guys popped him in
the snoot. Drug him off."

Jess quickly stood up.

"One of the guys yells at me: 'Tell them we're taking him
to the red house!' I heard something crack when they hit him
up side the head."

Jess laced her shoes up.

"What's the red house?" Blake asked, rising quickly.

"He going to bait me in there now. God, the way he
works. The strings. I've never seen so much blood in one
place. I wonder what's wrong with Cross?"

"I'm not following," Blake said.

"Smith's slaughterhouse," Jess replied. "They've taken
Alfbender to the butchery."

*Eleven o'clock. Raphael was hungry. He looked at the dry
furrows of skin underneath the operator's eyes. A couple of
busted capillaries. Red and blue. The operator was skinny
and shaking. Raphael was holding both of his wrists. Thaggart had taken Alfbender to the upstairs of the slaughterhouse.*

*"Your pulse is pretty high," Raphael said. He rocked the
operator by his wrists.*

"*What you going to do with me?*" *the man asked.*

"*What's your name?*"

"*Lugman.*"

"*Lugman, I want to run your machines some. Just a few minutes is all.*"

"*Yeah. That's fine. You let me go, though.*"

"*I hear you got new equipment.*"

"*Brand-new.*"

"*You don't use sledgehammers no more. You got a kind of gun, I hear.*"

"*A stunner. Electric. Yeah. Uh-huh.*"

"*How's it work, Lug?*"

"*Put it to their heads. Press the trigger like a pistol.*"

"*Oh, yeah. I see.*" *Raphael looked at Lugman's little neck and his long ears. He wanted to lick the man's nose. Too silly.* "*Now you got a fast heartbeat. Way too fast. You better take it easy. You might die. I don't want that. I just want your machines. Go talk a walk now.*" *He let the small wrists free.*

Lugman backed off. His chin jerked. His eyes were all pupils.

Raphael watched Lugman back away behind some animal pens, then he went up the wooden stairs. They smelled generously of blood.

Light up here in the narrow room. Levers and machines. A loading ramp leading into a holding pen. Two round-eyed calves waiting. The long silver pistol in a rack beside the shooting cage. The air full of calf urine. The hay breath of the calves. The humming of the machines. The nice light.

Alfbender stood face against the wall, Thaggart behind him. Raphael was worried about Thaggart. He didn't know how far the fellow would go.

"*Hey, Thag.*"

Thaggart jumped around. "*Damn! Why don't you make some noise!*"

"*Sorry. Go on downstairs. Look out for Jess.*"

"What the hell are you up to?"

"Just going to scare them a little. Don't you fret."

Thaggart aimed a finger at Raphael's chin. "I'm not part of nothing rough. Now I'm not. We're s'posed to take them home. I don't like all this other business."

"Go ahead on down now," Raphael said.

Thaggart moved toward the stairs. "How do you know she'll follow us here?"

"Just because, because, because," Raphael said.

"I'll be down there. I want to be out of this place quick. So get finished with your game, kid. Now you understand me?"

"I do, Thag. I surely do."

Thaggart quickly went down the stairs.

Alfbender started to turn.

Raphael laid a hand on his neck. "No, no. Just look at the ole wall now. You'll be alright."

"Why don't you ease up on us?" Alfbender asked.

"I don't know." Raphael slipped his hand into the cold steel handle of the stunner. "I've wondered, but I just don't know right now."

Blake smelled the slaughterhouse before they reached it. The odor was dull and thick. The building itself was made of cypress and painted red. It slanted out toward the river as if ready to dump its bloody work into the water. The length of its spine lay swaybacked, and the slate shingles shaled off unevenly. Four chimneys gargled flames and smoke into the air. At the end of the building small pipes and conduits drained rivulets of fluids and small portions of light into a dark canal. Blake stopped and looked up at the roof. He heard a crazing, a kind of dry-throated rasping: crows. He had seen them before, pacing there in the daylight. Now and again he could hear the crows let go a questioning cry. Their hard yellow feet clattered across the slate. From inside the building an animal screamed. The pens to the left of the house responded with glowing eyes which fixed on the great door before them. Hooves shuffled in the dirt. Horns and shoulders grated against wood. A hoarse groaning rumbled out from the pens and eyes turned red and wild by the night lamps.

Jess gazed up at the fire spewing from the chimneys.

"Alfbender's in there?" Blake asked.

"Maybe. Couple yellows?"

Blake gave her two. He had only six or seven left.

Jess swallowed them down, then found a side door.

Inside machinery clinked and clattered grimly above and below them. A little light glimmered from three small bulbs near the ceiling. The smell of blood. Blood waited like a presence.

"Alfbender!" Blake yelled.

A creaking came from above them, and Blake saw the first limp calf's body dangling about ten feet up.

"Alfbender!" he yelled again.

Jess pointed at a large vibrating machine which hung near the ceiling. She spoke in a dazed tone. "Press drop feeder to your left. Whole thing's automatic. Worked from the weight of the animal. They are stunned in the front room. Hooked in the noise. Hoisted up on the feeder, which trips the belt and the blades."

Blake took her hand. She buckled down on one knee. Her eyes looked bad.

Toward the back of the room began a purring, quick and light.

"Knifer," Jess said.

"I'm looking behind this machine," Blake said. He set Jess down against a support, then carefully moved ahead hands out before him. His eyes still had not adjusted to the darkness. He glanced back over his shoulder. The calf was slowly nearing the knifer. Some light caught in its numbed eyes. The nostrils and mouth trailed saliva, which fell into a gurgling trough beneath the feeder. Another body swung through the leather door. It was kicking, shaking the feeder.

"Alright, coolies, come and cut your barrister down," Alfbender said. He was hanging by his wrists. "These Birddogs have a few loose notions, friends." Alfbender spoke calmly though in short breaths.

Jess caught Blake by the ankle. "He doesn't know what's happening. Get up the ladder by the door. Try to pull him off when he comes by."

A light gleamed just above the ladder. Blake caught hold of the third rung and pulled up.

Alfbender took short breaths.

Suddenly the first calf seemed to wake. It kicked and began to writhe upon the hook in its nose. It drew its hindquarters into its belly. The hooves touched at the eyes.

Blake could feel the rust wringing off in his hands. Something cold was dripping on him from the ceiling. At the top of the ladder lay a platform. He tested it first, then eased onto the flat iron.

The calf began to moan and thrust its hooves at the hooks. The length of its thigh muscles bulged and contracted.

Blake could not reach Alfbender from the platform. "Too far!" he yelled.

"Try to get on the ledge," Jess returned. She was squatting, hands balanced upon the floor.

"Be cool," Alfbender said. "I'm alright."

The calf screamed out. Its mouth and nose poured blood.

Blake tried the bricks. They felt slippery but solid. He edged out onto them carefully. "Alf, how they got you fixed?"

"Two or three knots. Kick the metal clip above my hands."

The calf twisted only six feet from the knifer. Blake braced himself in a window casing. He decided to keep his right foot planted and kick with the left.

Alfbender's face had gone white; maybe he had not seen the knifer before. The blades were shining beneath the ceiling lamps.

70

"One good kick. That's all. Aim right at the metal above my wrist. Aim!" He jerked forward. The animal behind him kicked into his back.

The first calf hit a lever just before the blades: a loud mechanical clapping and coming together of metal. A large leather clamp slid about its neck. The head was pushed upward by a piece of steel. The body swung down even lower exposing the neck and belly. The calf swung over the deepest part of the water trough.

Alfbender had crossed his legs, drawn them toward his neck.

Blake was balancing on one leg trying to see if he could reach with a kick from the ledge.

The animal's body hit the rotary blades. A quick convulsion as the knife flashed in deep at the throat, then spun down the body neatly through the chest and intestines. The organs fell out, giving up steam. The eyes themselves still blinked a little as the black cavity of the calf moved beyond the blades toward other machines.

The air smelled sulfurous from the organs. Blake felt himself weaken. He tried not to look at the calf as it moved into darkness. When he turned to Alfbender he saw the lawyer was spotted in blood. He hung silently from the creaking belt.

Blake readied himself. He tried one kick and suddenly lost balance. His hold slipped on the casement. He felt his butt hit the ledge.

"For Christ's sake!" Alfbender yelled. "For Christ's sake!"

Jess shouted something from below.

Blake was scrambling to get back up. He couldn't get his feet back on the ledge. "I can't! I can't! Twist free!"

Alfbender began kicking. Blood ran from his wrists. He screamed out. The calf behind him bellowed and the other animal began to rouse and jolt the belt.

Blake tried again to find a grip. The brick wall was too slick. He got his heels as close as he could to the ledge and kicked up and back. One foot made the ledge, the other shot free. His hands missed the casement. "Alf!" He hit the floor hard on his right shoulder.

Overhead the belt bobbed and buckled. Both animals fought now.

Alfbender was just a foot or two before the knifer. He was straining away from the metal lever.

A snap and sparks broke out down the line. The calves fell when the belt broke. Then Alfbender went down just to the side of the water tank.

The knifer whined down slowly. The rest of the machinery began quieting down. Calves bleated along the floor. Blake unhooked one of the lawyer's legs still wrapped about the trough.

"It's okay. I'm okay," Alfbender said. His face was turning brown, clotted in blood. Blake ran to the shallow end of the tank and dipped some water. He wiped the lawyer's face.

"I'm telling you these guys are nuts," the lawyer said, holding his wrists against his jacket.

"Jess!" Blake called out. He ran to where she had been, but couldn't see her.

Alfbender limped up behind him.

Blake saw two doors leading out of the room. He pointed to Alfbender for the upper and he took the other. He picked up a wrench from the floor. "Are they here?" he asked. "Jesus, are they still in here?"

The lawyer crept into the shadows. He held a piece of pipe.

The next room smelled of decay. There was less light. Only one bulb overhead. Along the walls Blake could just make out trails of sea lichens and brown spots which appeared to be dried blood. The floor felt wooden and wet. It gave in to his feet.

Alfbender motioned at him. "Clean up there," he said.

"You think they got her?"

72

"Maybe," the lawyer said still pressing his wrists to his vest. "We search this place first. We play steady and cool."

Blake held up his fingers, turned his head, listening, to the left: a sound from just beyond the light's reach. High and whispering, almost like the wind. An airy noise somewhere ahead of them in the dark.

Alfbender put his hands out to his side as if to balance and stepped back to the upper part of the building.

Blake moved toward the windows on his right. At first he thought the river was making the noise, but as he approached, the sound became more quiet, finally ceased. He could hear something else now. Sobbing. Quiet and like a child's and somewhere below him. He felt a stickiness at his feet. One hand held the wrench while the other stretched before him. He felt as if something lay in wait for him in the dark. The palms of his hands felt only inches from something which kept pulling back, luring him further away from the light. Suddenly he stumbled and went down. His chin struck the floor and lights flashed in his eyes. He could smell blood over his face and hands now. Close to him he heard the sobbing again and a rustling. Somehow he had gotten the blood from the floor into his mouth. He thought about calling out but kept his sense. Crawling on his belly, he slid forward. Again the high whisper was rising. He tapped his fingers ahead of him, sifting through things, what he saw in his mind: pieces of bone, tatters of gut and hide, slivers of hooves, and traces of offal. Then there was nothing. He reached a hand out before him—only air. Easily he pulled himself to the edge of what seemed to be a large hole. Below him, the pit appeared to be six or seven feet deep. He could not see either end of it. About his face he felt something tickling, gliding like a web. Gnats were singing up from the pit and covering him. Quietly he tried to brush them away. Then he saw the first glimmers coming up from the dark below. At first he thought the light behind him was gleaming across a surface of water. He scanned intently and carefully hung his head down by the wall. The gnats came whispering up toward his face. He winced when one cold body wedged in his eye. He blinked it away, then heard the sobbing, louder.

"Jess!" he whispered.

A scurrying noise. Somewhere to the right he heard a cry. "Jess!"

"Help me."

"Where? Which way now?"

The scratching sound again.

"Get in, Buckles. You got to climb down, baby."

Edging his feet over the side his palms slipped. He fell only a couple of feet. The stench almost blocked his breathing. Taking the first few steps, he sprawled over the soft and irregular objects. They were spread all about him, many of them reflecting green and yellow light. He put his hands out to touch one. Most of it felt smooth, but at points rough and at other parts soft and liquid. He worked his way across the pit into a cove of light and looked down. Calves' heads. Eyes wide and white staring at him. The mouths agape and the blue tongues hanging out.

"Buckles," Jess whispered across the pit.

He spotted her squatting unevenly against a wall, arms wrapped about her shoulders. She did not flinch from the rats who rooted through the blood and hide. The calves' eyes seemed to be staring at him as he stumbled closer to her and finally got his arms around her shoulders. Jess did not move. No shivers, though now and again a queer sound rattled in her throat. Blake just held her for a moment, then yelled for Alfbender.

The lawyer found them quickly. Blake caught Jess by her arms and pushed her up toward Alfbender. Then he scrambled up the side of the pit and collapsed on the edge. The three of them stank and had the blood and gnats completely over them. Alfbender started to speak but stopped. Blake heard the rats still going and then Jess's belly rumbled. He held onto her and she hung her head and vomited into the pit. She finished and started to weep. They just all sat and looked back at the dully shining eyes and helpless mouths and bloody darkness below them.

"Where are they?" Blake faintly heard his own voice.

"One of them hung me up and turned the machine on. He must be outside somewhere."

Jess was trembling. She tucked her hands into Blake's.

The darkness and silence seemed complete. They sat tightly together on the edge of the pit. They could hear each other's breath in the silence. They did not speak.

Alfbender rose. "I'll slip outside. Get the cops."

"Go to Uncle Cross," Blake said.

"He's no good now."

"Cross will come get us," Jess said.

Blake stroked the back of her neck. His fingers settled in the roots of her hair. "Maybe we should all go out together."

"You let me move out the front. Listen real close," the lawyer said. "If you don't hear anything you'll know I made it. Then you and Jess leave through the side. Maybe I can draw them off."

Jess looked up at Alfbender. "Forget the police. Talk to Cross."

Alfbender leaned down toward them. "Okay, I'll see Cross. Just be careful and listen out for me." He squeezed Blake's neck and moved away.

They heard him open the door, but did not hear it shut. They listened toward the dark.

Blake laid the palm of his hand against Jess's stomach. Her abdomen contracted. "I'm scared," he said.

Jess silently pushed against him.

"You think he's okay?"

Her hand went over his lips. Waiting for a cry, a scuffle.

There was no sound.

"We'll make the side door, then get straight home. Does that sound right?"

"I don't know," Blake said. "I don't know."

They stood up and stepped carefully around the pit: a rotting smell, blood and membrane, the sound of their own footsteps, holding hands in the half light.

At the side door there was more light. Again they listened. Just silence.

"One thing," Jess whispered. "If they are there—if they're waiting, then we bluff. Never look weak. We bluff them. Remember, this still could be a game. Rough, but still a charade. Do you see?"

Blake opened the door and they crept onto the street.

They breathed the air by the river. Safe.

They put their arms around one another and said nothing.

At first Blake thought only the shadows of dinghies bobbed against the building before them. Then perhaps Alfbender and a friend. But the men came up too fast and too sure. One of them was holding a pistol. In the street both Birddogs looked lean. They smelled of sweat. Their eyes spent themselves carefully, tough and dry. The first one spoke easily, his voice soft and slow. He was holding the gun.

"Two steps backwards. You didn't say may I." Raphael smiled.

Jess had not seen them until the first one spoke. She flinched, then controlled. She hauled the young man in with a toe-to-eye glance. She reached out and tapped him on the chin. "Tag. You're it."

"I know," he said. His blond curls blew in the wind.

"Birddog, you got a pretty face," Jess said.

She sounded strong to Blake.

"You folks put some smart moves on my head tonight," Raphael said, still holding the gun low and straight. Thaggart kept quiet.

"I hear there's a rummage sale on brains at city hall. Maybe you could go on down and pick up something for yourself." Jess started to move ahead. Thaggart eased in front of her.

Blake kept still. He wasn't afraid, but he kept very still.

Jess locked her eyes on the pistol. "What you packing there, my friend?"

"A bad lick."

"What's your name?"

"Call me Raphael. This is Thaggart."

Jess moved her hand toward the pistol.

Raphael clucked his tongue but didn't move the barrel. "It's *real* bad on that end."

"Reckon?"

"Way down deep I know it."

Jess sighed and looked down at her clothes. "We got all this blood on us, Raphael."

Raphael shrugged. "It's alright."

"We should get this off," Jess said.

"We'll let you wash yourselves. It's a mess in there, I know."

"I could get you money," Blake said.

"No thanks," Raphael said.

Jess glanced at Blake. She seemed alright, almost playful.

"Cross doesn't like us to come home dirty. Oriental rugs and all. A little soap and water and there won't be a scene," Jess said.

Raphael stroked her arm with the pistol barrel. "Hi, Jess."

"Hands off."

"A little wart or something. Right in your belly button."

Blake thought to move slow with them. He was shaking now.

Jess was wiping some animal blood off her hands and onto her skirt. "Just get us to some water."

"Three small moles right at the bottom of your neck."

Jess stepped into the gun. "It's not loaded. Cross wouldn't

want baby sister blown bye-bye. Yep, I remember your eyes."

"You had a better bod then. You even had a little sun, lady."

"The lantern-jawed orderly."

"Somebody else I guess. You and me used to fingerpaint in therapy." He rubbed at his eye. "You got my cherry in the asylum. You didn't forget, did you?"

"We have to go now. It's quarter 'til twelve. We have to make that trolley," Thaggart said.

"Is there something you fellows need we could help you get?" Blake asked. Keep them talking. "I could get you a car."

"I like to walk. I like to feel my body, you know?" Raphael directed Blake forward and then Jess after him.

The trolley tracks were built up on wooden pilings which rose out of a brackish pool. Lichens and barnacles grew up the pilings' sides. Above, Blake saw the trolley car waiting. This was its final stop. The car's yellow light glowed within and then rolled over and out the full glass windows, spilling out onto the tracks and fading away into the dark just below the red wheels. Thaggart went up the steps first, and Raphael followed Jess and Blake. Jess was whistling all the way up: "Give me some men . . ." Raphael chimed in a few of the notes.

The wind came sounding from the east. An ocean wind. Blake wondered if Jess had seen the cartridges in the revolver. He had noticed the copper edges flashing when she had moved close to Raphael. Still, it could be a game, but Blake did not believe so. The guns *were* real, and the intent in Raphael's voice made Blake tremble just as much as the gun. The man spoke with a polite dullness, but there was this beat which came from his voice and the blinking of his dry eyes that was wrong. He carried the gun too well. He moved the pistol in his hands the way no real debit collector ever could. Still, Blake was not certain.

Raphael moved quickly to the conductor half asleep on his stool. He put the barrel under his jaw. "Off."

The conductor had his hat pulled over his eyes and a small chess set perched on his belly. He pushed his cap up and the barrel settled right down on his nose. "Oh shit," he said.

"You're right," Raphael said.

"I got maybe thirty bucks."

"Just step off the back here with me and you'll keep it all."

The conductor rose. The chess set clattered to the floor. Veins were blossoming across his nose. He took off his saggy hat and went to the back of the trolley.

Raphael followed him. "They say you got a photographic memory. Your friends say that."

"Oh no," the conductor said, his face tight and red. "I photograph. That's what they must have said. I photograph because I forget the past real quick. Memory like a tea strainer. Plain awful."

"Pawn to king four," Raphael said.

"That's funny. I play a little of that. We'd be good buddies at it. Come by when—you're finished."

"Pawn to king four," Raphael said again, a little closer to the conductor now.

Thaggart had moved Jess and Blake to the front section of the car.

"Pawn to queen three," the conductor said.

"Pawn takes pawn."

"Knight to queen bishop three."

"Nice," Raphael said. "I'm going on out with you and tie you down now."

"Please don't."

"You'll be able to get loose. I'm not trying to dismember you on the tracks, okay?"

The conductor walked forward into the dark. Blake heard them laughing a little, trading moves down the tracks. The quiet came up for a minute. Then there was a pop.

Thaggart was standing on the outside of Jess and Blake. He looked out the back door of the trolley.

Jess slapped her hands on the seat in front of her. "How long has that boy been collecting debits?"

"He's smart. Learned everything in a couple weeks. I told him he should go straight commission." Thaggart was nervous.

"He's a loon, Thaggart. Who picked him for this? He's been dropping bolts for the whole fifteen minutes I've known him."

Thaggart picked at a few hairs on a mole beneath his eye. "He's fitted out alright."

"What do you think that noise was—a damn maypop? He just blew that guy's brains across the river."

Blake felt his heart kick with adrenaline. He had heard the sound too. He knew that he must not allow Raphael to tie them up. He should go after him before that. He looked down and saw the river with a strange kind of sharpness as if his eyes had been cleared and now cut into the night with a cold edge.

Raphael entered the light of the trolley again. He stamped his feet and held the thirty-eight against his thigh. "Turn her on," he said to Thaggart. "We're dragging."

Thaggart was looking at him. He pulled a small length of rope from his pocket and tossed it on the floor. "How did you tie him up?"

Raphael glanced at the rope, then moved a hand to his jaw. A red tattoo, a strawberry gleamed on his little finger. "Cuffed him, Thag. Ironed him to some old nails. He'll get loose."

Jess leaned forward, closer to Raphael. "You told him a joke. Maybe exchanged opinions on queen pawn moves. You slugged him a couple times. Hung his head over the tracks and shot him."

"Not really," Raphael said.

80

"You murdered him."

"You got a bad imagination, lady."

Jess looked at him. It was a theatrical look. Protection. "You did some butchery back there."

Raphael squatted down close to her. Thaggart had opened the brakes and the trolley began grinding forward. Sparks were skating beside the tracks.

"I saw your husband on the stage," Raphael said.

"Once or twice I saw him when he wasn't," Jess said.

Blake's head was hurting. If he tried a move now, Raphael could shoot Jess easily. If there were bullets. No, but there were. He had seen the cartridges.

"He had something about him you could almost see. I felt better seeing him. He was reading the Passion."

"Is that man back there?" Jess asked.

"Sure."

"Alive?"

"He was afraid. I snapped one round off to show him the blanks."

"So when did you see my husband reading the gospel?"

"We were at the State Hospital Easter. You were there. He came and read it and I felt some real better."

"He just had a deep voice. Read anything to anyone in a deep, slow voice and they feel better."

"He was loving. He loved us by his voice and by his words. When he shook my hand, I felt it."

"You were the kid with the guitar. Blond hair. A lot longer and those real blue eyes."

Raphael smiled and propped the gun on his knee. The trolley was rocking now. The red seats and brass fittings were rattling along. The sea wind was pushing through the windows.

"I played the best ever back then. I was in Frisco at the beginning of everything and still had flowers in my hair when I came back here. I learned the songs that mattered and played them just for you."

"Always in C as I recall."

"I had no choice for me." He thumbed the gun's hammer. "Still don't have any really, man. No way to move but one now. See, I thought when we did it you were giving me something."

"You should keep things tidy about that. My son is here, and I think now to keep things neat all the way to the house is good."

Raphael searched the front tracks ahead. "You pull it over at the nearest station, Thaggart."

"No time."

"Fine, and just do it smooth because I have to use the bathroom. They need to shower too."

Jess made a quick move. Just as fast Raphael slapped one finger across her nose. Her head clipped back against the seat. A line of blood shot from one nostril.

Blake swung at Raphael and heard the blast and felt glass shattering all over him.

"I like guns and it's my business to carry them full of real shoot-'em-up stuff. I just put in a couple blanks for your brother," Raphael said very rapidly. He punched the gun into Blake's chest.

"Hold it down!" Thaggart was yelling.

Blake wiped the blood away from Jess's nose. She was doubled over into her knees. "There's no mistaking now. Dear God. Not now," she said.

"What's the station stop for?" Blake said, trying to keep his voice and eyes strong.

Raphael was taking him in from the sides of his blue eyes. His strawberried little finger stroked at his chin. "To get all that blood off. To let you get yourselves clean in there. Settle down now."

The trolley quickly traveled above the land. The Wheeler

Street Fair behind now, everyone still celebrating, dancing. The high walls of the roundhouse. The washed-out and weary city slums. When the harbor came into view, Blake felt the car braking down.

"Here. You pull off here," Raphael said, pointing to a station on the right-hand side of the tracks.

When Blake stepped out onto the ground the smell came straight at him. He could not see well at first. He helped Jess down. Thaggart went toward the station, which was made entirely of glass except for the base of the walls. He cut on a light inside. Behind him you could see the harbor and night boats working, and just beside the wharf, the clean-moving ferry, and beyond it, a yellow windowed house where people passed back and forth in costumes, and farther out, the breakers were going a ragged white and gray against the beach. Just to the side of the station door Blake saw the problem: a rotting pile of fish. Gold dollars they were called. Their sides were smooth gold up to the black of their backs.

Raphael went over and started kicking the fish into the sea. "It's an awful smell. That death. It rides me sometimes." He held one of the fish up. "Woosh, woosh," he said, moving the fish back and forth over his head. He flipped it into the dark. "You wonder who weeps for the fishes. You kind of wish somebody cared about the little life. Woosh, woosh in the waters. Woosh, woosh for the fishes gone to sleep."

Thaggart was puffing on a cigar.

"Thag, go on back and let that fellow up."

Thaggart poked the cigar into his mouth and walked up close to Raphael. "I thought you said he could work loose."

"I made him a promise not to get dismembered out there. That other trolley's coming. We're late, and I'm afraid he may be kind of too close to them tracks."

"You thinking alright, son?" Thaggart asked.

"Nice and neat."

Thaggart paused, flicked a little ash. He turned and gave

his cigar to Jess. "I think the shower's a good idea. I didn't intend all that butchery stuff, hon."

Jess took the cigar.

"Five minutes and I'll be back," Thaggart said to Raphael. He began walking back down the tracks.

Raphael pushed Blake and Jess into the station.

Jess was forced down into a chair. Her nose began bleeding again. Strands of hair dangled about her shoulders and her legs were spread out limply.

"You look finished," Raphael said.

Jess reached her hands up to wipe at her nose. She straightened herself in the chair.

"You can unbutton your shirt all the way down," Raphael said to Blake.

Blake had to make some kind of move.

"You remember that we did it, don't you?" Raphael asked.

"Screwed?" Jess said, her voicing hardening.

"I was seventeen. I thought—then I thought it was making love—but—screwed, yeah. We did that. I told you. You got cherries from me, you know?"

"I got crabs."

"You didn't talk so rough then, either. You had a niceness."

"So?"

"Just get clean now. All that blood stinks."

Blake had begun unbuttoning his shirt.

Raphael came over and finished the bottom three buttons and felt both of Blake's pockets. "I learned this a while back in a Salinas pool hall. You might have had something."

Blake closed his eyes. Then he looked toward Jess. Her face seemed out, so he switched his eyes to the harbor and felt his breathing slow, his heart too. Be calm. Somebody will come. This won't happen here. Not to you.

"You mind if I have a couple Valium before we get into the shower?" Jess asked. She dropped the cigar.

"You go ahead."

"Top left pocket," she said.

Raphael cautiously took the pills from her fatigue shirt.

Jess chewed them up.

Raphael untied Blake's shoes. "Take off your pants."

"No," Blake said.

"Oh, yeah. There's not a whole lot here now. I don't like to undress people, you see. So you go on now."

"I think if this isn't a game you'll lay a bullet right through my head. Do it," Blake said.

Raphael scooted back across the floor, his eyes retreating into the seams of his face.

"Blake, shut up!" Jess yelled.

"I don't have to leave your messy brains on the floor. I can hurt her, see?"

"Go ahead," Blake said. This time he was not going to wait. He could move out of this fast.

Raphael rubbed his earlobe into the barrel of his pistol. "You're a hard-ass. You don't know it, but you are. I knew that. You got all your family's tough genes." He moved behind Jess. He kept his earlobe in the pistol and took the flat of his hand and jammed her nose.

Jess screamed out. Blood rushed down over her mouth. Her legs twined together.

"Christ!" Blake yelled and jumped toward her. The gun came down to the side of her head.

"Yeah, yell real loud for Him. That's who she took away from me. Me standing here so damned with you. She took my cherry and something more."

Jess was leaning over her knees sobbing and trying to stop the bleeding.

"Let me help her," Blake said.

Raphael nodded.

Blake pushed her hands apart. One nostril seemed split.

Raphael gave him a handkerchief. Blake placed it over her nose and held her.

"Go ahead and help her off with the clothes. She lost some blood on that shot. She'll be spinning."

Blake embraced her tightly. "You alright?" he whispered. He felt her nod. "You . . . does it hurt?"

"Not—" She coughed and spat out a mouthful of blood and phlegm. "Not too awful much," she said in a tiny voice.

Ralphael tapped Blake on the head. "Break, break. One, two, three . . ."

"Jesus, what have we done? Where did all of this come from?"

Jess sucked in the lower part of her lip, shaking her head.

Raphael started to peel away her stained shirt.

Blake slashed his hands away.

Raphael moved backward.

Blake looked back at Jess. "Mama, you're going to have to hold your arms way up."

Shakily Jess raised her arms halfway. Blake pulled them over her head and slipped the shirt up to her wrists. A blade flicked through the sleeves, and the blouse came off in Blake's hands.

Raphael was holding the file-pointed shaving razor against his shoulder. "Get them all off her now. I know this ain't so easy for any of you here. It's going to be tough."

Blake pulled off her skirt and shoes. The animal blood had soaked through to her slip, and now some of her own blood made the material soggy.

"See how it begins to take something away from her? Threads hold part of our souls. Everything matters."

Blake thought about trying to rush him, make any kind of movement, but Raphael was holding the pistol straight down on the top of her head.

"Why don't you just go ahead with us?" Blake said.

"Want you clean."

"Why?"

"Squeaky like little rubber ducks."

"Any reason at all?"

"When we laid together, me and your ma, we were as clean as two bars of soap. White and slick. I lost my chance at paradise squeaking across her belly in the Quiet Room." He pointed to Blake's belt buckle. His face seemed rich and slow and sad.

Blake's trousers fell to the floor. He scuffed off his shoes.

"I can finish myself," Jess said. "How about that for me?"

"See, I wanted him to go ahead and do it."

"I don't think I was so cruel to you."

"You better go over it again, lady."

"There's just a few more things left. He doesn't know how. It would be too hard on him."

Raphael laid the gun against his cheek. "You take them off, then."

Jess stood and pulled away the last of her clothes.

Keeping his eyes away from her, Blake felt his face go cold.

"Let's go ahead and rinse all that nastiness off in the shower right away," Raphael said.

Jess folded her arms over her breasts and stepped into the stall. She was shivering. The water thundered out of the pipes. She gasped and pressed herself against the back wall.

"Don't you have some hot water for her?" Blake asked.

"Nope. You squeeze on in." Raphael moved beside the shower and pointed the gun against the metal wall just at Jess's waist.

"We don't go in together."

"Mother and son all squeaky together."

"No."

"This will do something for you, maybe. I was like her son. I loved the lady like that at first."

"What are you trying for here?"

87

" 'Loving is the beginning of immortality'—Plato. I knew that before I read him."

"The gun won't work for you that way." Blake began moving toward Raphael.

Raphael cocked back the hammer. "It'll go off in a second."

"She'll be safe then."

"Soft nose mean anything to you?"

"Not now."

The blade came out of the dark window just behind Raphael and silently pressed against his throat.

"Sharp as shit," Thaggart said.

Raphael did not move his eyes or the gun.

"Down now."

"You really that kind of hard, Thag?"

The knife dug a little. Some blood rose.

"Bad apples I culled all my life," Thaggart said.

The muscles under Raphael's eyes jerked. He lowered the thirty-eight.

"Pass that pistol on back here," Thaggart said.

The gun came to him through the window.

"Now the shiv."

Raphael handed the razor over his left shoulder.

Blake leapt forward and struck Raphael in the face, then kneed him in the belly. Raphael fell against the shower. Blake cut off the water, grabbed Jess's skirt and handed it to her. Thaggart was tying Raphael to a pipe.

When they had finished dressing, Blake helped Jess to pin up her damp hair. She was still trembling, but the Valium was walling up her eyes. Thaggart pulled out a bottle of vodka. He had given Jess his shirt. Blake took a swallow, then put the bottle to Jess's lips. She had two long drinks, then moved to where Raphael was tied down. "Even tonight in the middle of everything, I wanted to say I was sorry. I was unhappy in there. You were pretty and young. I didn't know you had commitments. You had such cool eyes. I thought it was all old stuff to you. I'm sorry."

Raphael shuffled his legs across the floor. His eyes were still and dazed.

"I'm taking you two home now. I'll get the cops back for him," Thaggart said. He led Jess to the trolley.

Blake waited inside. "I ought to bust your jaw. Leave some mark on you."

"Maybe so."

"I should really do something to you for this. I feel that duty someway. It wouldn't be hard for me to blow your head apart. It wouldn't hurt me and I could do it. Maybe I should."

"It might be better," Raphael said.

The trolley began rolling outside.

"See, I know it would be better. Just to blow you away would be the right thing."

"Move one way real hard."

"Yeah," Blake said. "Both of us know it's the right thing to do. I wonder why, though." He went out and got on the trolley, now picking up a little speed.

Blake sat beside Jess. Her eyes were shut and she moved closer to him. Her nose had swollen some. He rested his head against hers. He felt alone and failed and inconsequential.

The trolley bucked down to the flat city lights. At the first station Thaggart stopped the car. The third shift driver was waiting. He asked questions and Thaggart told him to drive and that there had been some trouble, but things were copacetic now. When Thaggart got off he looked back and said, "I'm really sorry. I didn't know about all this craziness. Don't worry about Raphael. I'll get the cops right to him."

They pulled away and moved by the squares and revolutionary monuments and the Georgian houses of beveled glass windows and stylish broken stucco and raw brick. Blake knew his mother's mind, even now. She saw all that passed as a stage setting, though nonetheless real: downtown old money. Respectability and worth. Parties flourished in the homes. The front stoops of wrought iron, the steps of yellow marble were cluttered with costumed drinkers and black waiters. Trellised gazebos held ruddy pots of camellias and coiffed grande dames who sipped cherry and kept count of the hostess's number of drinks. Their flint-jawed husbands tossed down Wild Turkey neat and fit two fingers into their vests, talking politics and duck hunting.

Several stops farther on. Few people rode. Mostly winos. Rutted foreheads, dirty necks, and ashen hands. Common people, as Jess would say, and she intended no malice, only distinction. Then the car swept up the trestle and over a stretch of trailer parks and gas stations. Finally they reached the great marsh.

The moon was still high. Looking down into the marsh Blake saw the first stand of cypress. Here the night stood darkest and best, supported by the enormous trunks of cypress and their canopy of leaves and an even deeper dark waiting beneath the limbs. Beyond them the weaker forms of scrub oak and swamp maple rose from a threading mist, and the first tidal channels cut into the lighter color of marsh grass and the barren white of cattails: a place of desolation. Of rotting piers and lonely glades. Pools of stagnant water, briers, sink holes, and the sick dampness of lichens and mildews. Blake was seeing the marsh as if for the first time: confused by the hundred different paths and unable to mark his way by the tendrils of black water unknowable and silent, flat as the veins of the dead.

The car blew sparks into the marsh and stopped at a ramp on the edge of Cane Island. Below them Blake saw the lighted hand bridges and pavilion of the state park. His family had given the land as a tidal sanctuary. They had sold off three large lots on the island, paved a street, and put up lamps.

Blake helped Jess off. She was dazed under the Valium.

They walked down the new road toward the house. His spine was aching and he felt weak. Around a curve of mulberry trees they stopped.

Blake and Jess stood before the Victorian house, watching as if they expected something from it. To Blake it did not seem smaller like so many other places returned to, but if anything immense as an endless dream, and as divided in its nature as the play of any opposites. A place that knew you as well as you knew it. A clean pocket of space and pride where the latest sleeps are as sound and pure and silent as the first, and where all sounds and odors and lights sail through you as friends passing faithfully the last watch in the night. A second feeling arose which Blake knew Jess felt much more than he: a tactile sense of dread. Once more he imagined her thoughts as she was silent. Home places, besides harboring the smell of favorite quilts and chimneys twinkling with the friendly tunes of wind and stars, held too all the finest tools for torture. Here as in no other fast or slow plane of being could you be bound and slowly disjointed, fractured into weakness and fumbling. Homes were sugared gingerbreads and chocolate-pudding plots. Homes and the near-abiding, teeming blood of kin ruled in you, even in your dreams like the awesome God of Sinai, demanding appeasement and respect and wariness from first light to the last lamp. Here where you let your fists slip away from your head and eyes, from your heart, could the cruelest traps be sorted out and laid for you in daylight conversations on verandas or in the first hearty hellos of your own kin answering the door late in the evening.

Cross opened the door evenly. His face came across broad and healthy, the maple hair just frosting, the pupils of his eyes moving like violets. He went straight by Blake and caught Jess by her arms and pulled her into more direct light.

"Damn, sister. How the hell did you get that cut?"

Cross swept them quickly in and locked the thick stain-glassed door behind them. His golden lab—Munson—stared at them from the library.

Blake felt his body nearly lurch out for his uncle. "Raphael!" he wanted to scream. "Raphel tried to kill us. It just happened. This man tried to murder us!"

But now, in the house again, the learned timing of years held him back. He said nothing now, though his veins spread to tell the story, to warn: There is no more safety. Raphael.

Cross had a polite gut for a man fifty-four and six feet two. His wrinkles spread manageably. He widened his feet and bent one knee. He picked up his cloisonné cup and sipped at his coffee. A tight squint came up in his left eye and a low cigarette smile weighed out across his mouth. "Beer-hall brawl?" he asked, studying Jess's face.

Jess seemed to gain a quick supply of posture. She crossed her arms and tilted her head, tossing out a stare (she had the squint around her eye too, a family trait). "When I shot pool and won and fought bums for quarters, did anybody ever scratch this face?"

Cross held onto his stare, rocking a bit on his heels, the left eye nearly blind now from the squint. "I smell whiskey."

"Because your nose ain't busted open."

"She needs to rest," Blake said, glancing at Munson. He had sprawled back to sleep.

Neither brother nor sister moved.

"I don't want you drunk in the house."

"You don't want me sober outside of it."

"You've been taking pills again."

"I'd wade in them up to my knees to shake off the Bird-dogs."

They were quiet a moment. Eyes judged the potency of eyes.

"You in pain?" Cross asked.

"Just about."

"I don't like the looks of that nose."

"I was always passionate about yours."

"Busted up but still joking."

"Come give sister a billy-goat-gruff kiss."

Cross relaxed some and let loose the squint. He sighed and went over to her cautiously. Bending his face delicately to hers, he kissed her on the cheek.

"Very well," Jess said, again seeming to be weak. She twined her arm around his. "Tend to sister now. I've popped something loose up here and it hurts."

Cross and Blake helped her down the dark hall and into the hunting pantry.

The hunting pantry was painted white and had a red-tiled floor. The room shone wholesomely and gave itself to you in old wooden cabinets encased in screens and jars crammed tightly with summer fruits and preserves. The walls were cluttered in black pans and stashes of wooden spoons. On the door hung calendar pictures of fishing villages and hunting scenes: mounds of partridges, a prime dead hare, the taut body of a deer gutted and hanging from a golden tree. The aroma lay here the same as it had in the days of his grandmother. That time suddenly rushed back to him, of cinnamon cookies and whole-wheat flour, of honey and raisins and—despair. Blake had not been able until just now to name the feeling. Despair lingered here open to the senses, not exactly tangible, but rather like the feeling and sight and smell of an empty coal grate or the lonesomeness of seawater caught in a slim prison of rock. He remembered that, younger, he had sensed it too, this feeling of vulnerability, a complete need to be infused by some strength and resilience that had somehow passed away and could not be produced by your own being. Here in the pantry, cookies and all sweetbread confections rushed to your comfort. In the dining room, where the cold tea-kettled heater blinked the blue pilot flame, sound silver and white-faced china and splendid carved chairs rescued you, and likewise through the whole house each room trucked out its booty to assure you of your longevity and esteem. It seemed to Blake that all of these things had been left to promise those here that they were not unloved. And that particularly here before these objects of dust and devotion, holding close to one of your own kin, you had always a bearing and a clear path through the waters, always a light upon the table and a bordered plate waiting your return—and your surrender.

Cross took care of Jess's cut. Their talk began slowly.

Blake set an ancient family bowl in his lap. The outside still had tree bark on it. The inside was pine yellow and had white wavering rings. He picked up the creaking nutcracker and the small pike. He listened to their conversation now and muffled the sound of bursting pecans with his palm. He picked out the meat and tried to be patient.

Jess related how for four hours they had been chased about town by the Birddogs. Incredulously to Blake, Jess and Cross laughed about this now, sitting together, holding hands on the sofa. Blake sensed that the laughter was sincere, that it came up from them through a knowledge that seemed pitiable to him as he watched them looking back upon themselves, upon the utter sadness and travesty of this evening and many other evenings as well, detached from their own hearts and bodies, becoming only laughter and intellect while embracing each other's plight and realizing that neither could act any other way, each one separate and determined, though his uncle's path was more merciless perhaps. In this kind of examining it could be said that his mother had not revealed a selfless, sustaining mercy either. Her running, her attempt at freedom was done not without guile: such freedom would condemn her brother to misery, a quality of refined dispossession. In such light both of them were without an unblemished compassion, and realizing this (and maybe more elements that brother and sister feel when unarmed and close

together), they laughed until tears came to their eyes re-
counting the tales of past plots and escapes while behind all
of the acts stood the real fear of both of them, for now
tolerated and understood: Jess was preparing to leave.

As they listened to one another, hugging once in a while,
becoming serious at points, nodding their heads in apprecia-
tion of certain feelings generated by the acts of the other,
Blake sensed at the base of their objectivity a long, trundling
brook of sorrow—grief for what one had done to the other, of
what one would continue to do to the other, sorrow for the
other's pain and consummate unhappiness and for one's own
pain too, and beside that remorse a form of contrition that
came to their eyes and faces at some memory recalled too
vividly, so that detachment slipped away and the body
twitched from the pain. Blake did not have to analyze. He
simply saw these things. He knew them.

A quiet came to the conversation for a time.

Blake passed out some pecan meat. Cross and Jess took the
dry halves almost shyly and whispered thank-yous. They
were resting now. His uncle pressed business lips together,
blinked his eyes in meditation and exquisitely slipped a hand
inside his coat as if adjusting papers. His mother fitted four
fingers to her cheek and looked at her brother with baby-
sister eyes.

Cross tilted his head back against the wall and folded his
white hands in his lap. He continued and said humbly, as if in
confession not only to his sister but to himself and Blake as
well, that he had had her followed because he loved her and
feared for her to leave town, especially since she had begun
drinking again. Then he pushed deeper into himself, saying
(with a bitter-fruit smile and coarse voice) that maybe he
simply wanted her to remain there with the family like always and have those hot teas and brandy-cake sessions of
gossip and new books read and never be apart through the
whippoorwill nights. Finally his face became grave. His

hands slid boyishly beneath his armpits as he accused himself in yet another voice of something darker and that perhaps everything he had said was wrong and deceitful and that maybe he simply wanted to hurt her for a reason he was not sure of at all.

Jess took his hands and in a comforting voice whispered that the darker part was probably not true, or if it was the case she too had found herself meddling about in the blacker parts of herself, and that these little forays into the shadow's lair had to be expected in a host of otherwise beneficial acts.

Again there was a lull, and Blake thought that each had acquired a temporary absolution from the other. His uncle had obviously opened himself wide and received his sister's consolation. His mother by forgiving had declared her own guilt and momentarily rid herself of it. But to Blake each seemed to be looking beyond pardon and sympathy toward some method of assuring themselves that they were not monsters and that just possibly they had a completeness that could not be attacked and digested by each separate act that was committed. They were in need of something that would allow them to say that, yes, acts hurt and bring up welts and wounds, but I understand—no, rather, I do not understand, but I accept as much as my sanity will allow these errors against me and hold them as a mystery, knowing as I do that you *do* love me no matter your acts. Damn the act. Because I know that potential stands much nobler than act, for act lies absolutely consequential to far too many variables and considered by itself betrays and suborns what we essentially —we in a pristine state, unaffected by our own chemistries, morphologies, greeds, and fears—are. They wished to say we will never again consider acts as the definition of ourselves but rather study the entire body of our being and realize that only through this perception can we allow ourselves an estimate of our own goodness or evil. By acts alone we will never know ourselves.

So now brother and sister sat hand in hand, having gone through most of the evening romp. Jess had carefully left out the slaughterhouse and Raphael. Blake knew both would come up in the evening at the time when she needed them. There now climbed between his uncle and mother the silence that precedes a walling up of self again. Soon their hands unlocked. Masks cinched themselves into position through a more careful choice of words and cold ballet of eyes. The silence began to strengthen and both knew there was nothing to stop this attrition until the last lace was tied about their jaws, the last stone laid into place in their faces. The time of peace between them was over again. Blake could feel them preparing now, readying themselves for what they had to do.

Cross got up from the sofa, his face already taking on the business of this evening—his life and survival. He pushed his hands into his stately suit pockets and secured his eyes from any feeling. "Well, we do have a little supper waiting, I think. The cook stayed late."

Despite the residue of alcohol and pills, Jess seemed fresh about her face, and her eyes had acquired a snappy punch. "How nice. You knew we would be dropping in. Prescience?"

"Concern," Cross returned.

"My, my. We've entered into the lists again, haven't we, dear? I can see the armor coming down and the bright ax beaming in your eyes." She placed a finger on her chin.

They stood across from one another and had resolution on their faces. Blake still sensed between them (though you could not see it) a smile, a knowing. He had felt the same kind of humor pass between his father and mother just before their battles. When he was young he had been terrified of this presence, since it always heralded a psychological dismantling. Now he was surprised to feel a guarded excitement and curiosity.

Cross gave a faint nod and left the pantry for the dining room.

Jess winked at Blake.

He pointed at her nose. "Did he fix you up?"

A small bandage pinched her left nostril. "He has a peculiar sense of healing." She smiled.

"You should go straight to Cross and tell him about Raphael. About what happened out there."

"I thought so when I first came in." She looked out a window. "But I think now, just to wait and play Cross out."

"Raphael was going to kill us," Blake said.

"It seemed so. God, it surely felt that way."

"No. He *was* going to shoot us. He hit you. He had a loaded gun."

"Loaded pistols do not a murder make," Jess said, still looking into the dark.

Blake cupped his hands behind her elbows. "You knew he was ready to blow us both away. You absolutely knew that, looking at him."

"Looking at him I did know it—then. But now Raphael lies out there and we are here, and I cannot say what he really intended."

"You were in the asylum together. He has something against you."

"I've been behind the bricks eleven times now, Buckles. There were, I'm afraid, a lot of blue-eyed boys who played guitars, and I was always lonely and looking for favors."

"He's mad."

"Holding the gun, he was mad."

"Another game, then. Cross's game, and one of his Bird-dogs became hysterical. Nothing more than that?"

Jess turned to him, her face very alive, very sure. "Well, when he gets both feet in the trough tonight we'll look behind brother's ears and see how much dirt there is."

"If I had the pistol, I might have killed Raphael."

98

"You *might* have. He *appeared* mad. The time *seemed* violent. Now we are safe here in our home where we longed to be. And supper's waiting."

Her complete confidence and irony confused Blake. He stuck his hands into his pockets.

She smoothed his hair. "Now both of us must change clothes and bathe. We should not attend the table bloody since we will probably be leaving that way. Tonight I have to pin Cross to the mat so we can make that train by seven. You are about to be blooded. They'll set to break you down. Cross and Millis know I'm ready to leave, and they'll use everything against us. Get yourself ready now. Call out some discipline. It's going to be hard tonight."

She left the room.

Blake felt as if his mind was not perceiving things. What had happened in the dark station had been real. Raphael had intended harm. Hell, he was going to kill them. He had it in his eyes, his hands. How could she simply move into the sphere of this house and say that it had all been an illusion? Of course she had not said that exactly. She had said she could not tell now whether they were actually about to die or not. She could not see behind Raphael's eyes. She did not know (yet) how hard Cross was working at them through the Birddogs. Raphael *was* a Birddog. Blake stood amazed at himself. He had been convinced that they were about to die, but as soon as his mother interpreted the incident, drew it through her mind and spoke gently and serenely, he found himself reversed, or at least unsure.

The hall clock chimed twelve-thirty. Blake's head was hurting again. Maybe food would give him some pluck and these things, all the byzantine elements and ruses of the evening, would fade and be handled with potatoes and gravy and the dinner sortie that was building. As he went toward his bedroom, the house popped and tuned itself like a ship loading ordnance.

Blake combed his wet hair straight back just outside the dining room. He peeped through the glass doors. The room had never been wired for electricity, and the candles of the chandelier showered the wainscoting and the ornate molding and the white walls. The east side wall was glowing like a forest: Stained glass climbed from its carved base seventeen feet high, and for twelve of those feet in the center of the glass flamed an immense and naked seraphim whose face and feet covered themselves by iridescent and fiery-eyed wings, the rest of his body being bare and sinewy flesh. About his wings lay deep-red roses and violets (in between these gleamed the shrewd eyes of lizards and toads), while behind and above him towered trellises burdened in fruit—bananas, cherries, pineapples, and oranges. The angel himself held one hand out toward a man much smaller, who sprawled apparently lifeless upon a bank of fruit. Near the top of the glass, painted in silver letters, was the aphorism: ACORNS "IS" DIAMONDS IN YOUR OWN BACKYARD.

Blake could see supper completely covered the sideboard. The food steamed in old china and crystal and chafing dishes. A stone pot of coffee nearly browned the room in its dark aroma and beside it a serving dish of pudding was banked high in whipped topping. At the very head of the board, minioned at its base by watercress and rude Irish potatoes split and stuffed with cheese and butter, reigned a two-foot round hump of beef, slowly dribbling juices from its browned exterior. Blake imagined at its center sat a heart cold and bloody and uncuttable.

His uncle's meals had always been simple.

It seemed to Blake that the initial steps of warfare had always begun at these kinds of meals, as if it were unseemly to launch attacks before a bowl of soup or a meat-loaf sandwich. His family needed the moats of pudding and potatoes, sauces and fruits from which they could derive a feeling of splendor and power, even a quality of savageness. There were at least three occasions Blake could remember when his mother had been committed somewhere between the serving of the salad (which for some reason they had in the middle of the meal) and the spooning up of desserts. For his family, then, meals, even those not nearly as pompous as this one, bordered the time when you must keep every weapon close and at the ready, when you judged each sentence spoken as to its actual intent and meaning, careful never to expose your own feelings about some recent subject that you found delightful, knowing that such ingenuousness would provoke their descent upon you.

Blake pushed his face against the cool glass, studying them. His uncle appeared immaculate and warm, flush-faced in his tweedy suit. His Aunt Millis smiled rubily, her yellow eyes dizzy but hunting, her little fingers exquisitely raised like palps upon the table. Jess seemed relaxed, her neck high and white below the sharpest eyes, the dampness of the shower still gleaming at her temples. Polite, incredibly agile, and seductively innocent in their inquiries on one another's health, cares, and the happenings of the day, Blake knew that they had already begun probing. With each question and feathered response they sounded out any new strengths, and of course they awaited any sign that betrayed a new weakness, a tiny blister or tear that could be worked upon in the time after the meal. Suppertime, then, was mostly a period of simple reconnaissance and assessment of resources, unless someone lost his footing and made a straightforward statement that brought short, quick blows from every table setting: a tick of an eyebrow, the ring of a spoon upon crockery.

These elaborate suppertime exercises had seemed ridiculous, contemptible, and witty to Blake, except when they had directly involved either of his parents. Tonight, however, he knew that they would search one another with piked and glinting seriousness and intend as they had not before to garrote and cudgel until Jess had been broken to stay or until she prevailed over them. Blake knew that if his aunt and uncle could find her balance during this meal, just the right setting of her mind, that later they would be able as they had in the past to pitch her neatly back into the family, where Blake believed they accomplished two purposes: One—she was still with them, sustaining, absolutely recoverable and able to secure their lives again and elucidate their earthly purpose. Two—they were able to sate the sibling desire to avenge themselves upon her for those moments during the fray when she stung them hard.

Tonight Jess would have to use all her guile—sweetness, dishonor, integrity, treachery, and optimism—in order to break through and pass them. They would demand her best performance as they gave their own. Blake knew her mind could sweep through them like a scythe through straw. They of course knew this as well and so would not try wits with her as much as go for something lower and more instinctive: an emotion, the unearthing of some past guilt or pain. But Blake was convinced of her strength and that tonight Jess was determined to leave—to meet the train by seven and finally begin to create a worth, a health for herself and for him, too. For Blake had come to see that a mother's happiness was as necessary for her son during his later life as during his encapsulation in her womb. When her eyes beamed sound and her hands moved in a sure and slow grace and her voice rode the day and the night as smoothly as the new moon, then he too felt of use and at command.

Blake pushed open the door to the dining room with deference. He nodded slightly to his uncle and mother and kissed his Aunt Millis on the cheek. His aunt asked some silly questions about school and he returned the appropriate answers and sat down at his place. The room was bleeding in candlelight, the seraphim, sparkling fruits, aromas of food. The minds of those at the table popped like copper rods. Blake listened to the beginning banter and then found himself rising in feeling. Before, he had thought the emotion was the simple expectation of food. Now he knew that his heart geared high and his humor improved not because of the sauces and dessert, but because he yearned to compete. Here he could defend his mother. Here he could win a part of this little empire of hurts and appeasements, victories and compromise: Here was the quest. Sitting at the table now, he felt one clear center to him: to beat his aunt and uncle, taking them on at the most dangerous and their most powerful place—the supper table at home.

Cross looked easily at Blake across his steaming cup of coffee. "Well, I'll start the cheese, and I think tonight Blake can carve the roast."

Blake went to the sideboard and picked up the carving knife and fork.

"We heard about your Halloween show at that bar," Millis said gingerly. Her red fingers played along the plate. Her red glasses hung matronly by silver chains upon her bosom.

"Just one night," Jess said, taking a piece of cheese and passing the plate down.

"We're glad you could come tonight," Cross said.

"How could we turn down such lovely invitations?" Jess said.

"We just wanted you here, Jess. You and Blake," Millis said.

"For how long?" asked Jess, her eyes getting smart.

"A while," Millis said. The fat little fingers raised defensively.

"My life? My son's life?"

"To eat a little late supper with us. To be a family," Cross said.

"We'll dig a little pudding with you, then beat it."

"A tryst?" Millis asked.

"Oh, Millis, you've been reading again. What a nice word. No, not a tryst. A dream. I catch a dream at seven."

"Along the bone now," Cross said and rose to direct Blake.

"Last night I was reading something Freud had to say about dreams. 'The pig dreams of acorns and the goose of maize,' " Millis said.

"How about the hinny?" asked Jess.

"Mr. Freud did not comment upon—the hinny."

"Perhaps hinnies don't dream."

"I should think they do," Millis said.

"Of what?"

"Fodder, I suppose."

"Oh my, has Mother not appeared in your dreams lately?"

"What?"

"Do you know what a hinny is, sister?"

"A hybrid. A mule."

"A eunuch."

"Coarsely put."

"Able to plant seed, though never to bear it."

Millis tried to cover the sting. "But you know, if he's right, if they do dream at night, I wonder . . . do they dream of their own end? Or their mate's?"

"I could go on a while about butcheries, here and there."

"We never saw you weep for him. You should have cried just a little. He *was* your husband," Millis said.

"In some ways he was more your husband. I just stood in for the marriage and out with the kid. You managed the pots and pans and treachery."

"My heart never betrayed you."

"Your heart? Oh yes, that—I'd forgotten. It seems every time I get a peek, the cold little darling sees its shadow and burrows again. Your heart, Millis, heralds a winter of betrayals."

"Your husband—"

"Never betrayed me. Never."

"He cheated."

"Only at dominoes and women. One went down as easily as another. And just as importantly to him."

"I never hurt you," Millis said.

"Let me see. I wonder how much of my brain you managed to burn out? One ounce? Two, perhaps? Heavens, maybe a whole cupful of frontal lobe lumped like Sunday's oatmeal."

"Jessica," Cross said.

"Oh yes, mustn't ruin that charming hunk of bloody meat. How many children did the new neighbors have?"

Then they all heard it. Blake turned suddenly toward the hall door. The roar came from outside, in the dark: a deep rolling phlegm from the chest and grinding together of jaws. Silence.

Millis and Jess looked toward the windows.

"Some child," Jess said. "Some trickster."

Millis's voice was unsure. "It sounded too harsh to me. It sounded like something wild."

"Munson," Cross said. "He has a cold. Makes him sound much worse than he is." Cross smiled. "Keeps the goblins away."

He served the meat and the rest of the food. They ate quietly.

Placing concerned fingers on his double chin, Cross pushed away a partly finished plate. "Business is going well. Picking up. You should have seen me, Jess. Why, just two days ago they patched me into three cities. Chicago, Denver, L.A. I was burning up the dimes. Had to fight a table-L rating and cancer of the prostate, but I got the paper on him—two hundred fifty thousand straight life."

"Tough, I bet," Jess said, looking at him softly.

"Well, I don't have it for sure yet." He reached to his left and poured some coffee and lit up another cigarette. The cloisonné cup sparkled. "I mean, she'll go through if the raters don't go nuts. But even then . . . Well, they won't be burying us all in silver caskets. Ten thousand bucks, maybe. Enough to make repairs on the house."

Jess reached across the table and played at his sleeve. "You always had the charm. The sunshine. Why, you could pipe bees from the hive in the death of December," Jess said.

"I understand your dream. I do. But if you could make arrangements about your interest in the house, in case there was a tragedy," Cross said.

"Home," Jess said, almost silently. "Keeper of hearts. Big cookie box of bangles and bows; of all things broken and mended."

"We don't want to lose our home. If something happens to you out there, we don't want to risk that. You could sign something," Millis said.

"A will?"

"I think it's appropriate."

"Aunt Millis, you're a bitch," Blake said.

Cross clinked his spoon against his cup. Millis ruffled her napkin.

"Too crass, love. Easy. Move very easy," Jess said.

Blake felt himself blush. He had blundered. Too hard and too much to the point. His family possessed an oblique grace, never looking exactly where they punched, keeping their eyes and words just off the center. Chastened, he fit his napkin into his belt.

"No will," Jess said. "That's nasty, I suppose, but—no. I'll take my interest with me."

"Thievery, sister," Millis said.

Jess placed a hand carefully on the side of her neck. "Tell me, Cross, is Millis—that is, does she still go to the local porn flicks for the Saturday matinee? About three A.M. in raincoat and galoshes, as I remember."

Cross looked at Millis, who straightened her shoulders and joined her hands.

"Physically you never seemed to *entirely* fit in there. All those slobbering cripples popping pimples in their stubble."

"Stop it."

106

"What is it, Millis? The screwing? Do you go to watch penetration? Or is it simply for camaraderie? Or perhaps just to see the lame bemused by pretty pictures while you listen to belt buckles ring against the floor like dimes."

Millis rose from the table, the pockets beneath her eyes red and swelling. "You're monstrous."

"Poor hinny," Jess said. "Poor Millis." She turned to Blake and took his head in her hands. "Do you know I can still remember when he first bucked in me like a new lamb. Look. Look at his fine eyes and shoulders, sister. Now when you go to your bed tonight and intrigue yourself, just remember that your body will never swell, will never kick with anything more than gas and the night's lodging of snaps and pot pie."

Millis was creasing her napkin, fingers stiff as her face.

The hall rumbled again as the scream rolled in from the outside and rattled a pane in the leaded glass.

They sat together in the silence.

Part Two

As Blake followed his uncle from the dining room he felt afraid. He knew fairly well what this move was to acquire. Divide and conquer. If Cross could keep mother and son separated, then he could work fastidiously against their weakest veins and impulses. Alone with either of them, Cross could set his jaws, lick his lips, and lay out the stakes.

Blake tried to stop these thoughts. It was his uncle who walked before him now. His own kin. His uncle who had taken care of him, preserved him from the violence of that time when the space that lay between his parents' eyes was like a meadow blasted and cratered and suffocating. Blake found himself remembering an attachment for the man now, not love but fondness. Too many nights when his parents had laid siege to one another Cross had creaked up the stairwell and brought his nephew diversion and comfort.

Even on Christmas Eve they fought. Christmastime. His wide windowed room, frost upon the panes. The bustling fire and red stocking. The smell of burning hickory wood and niggertoes and tangerines. The screaming and loud hatred of his parents fighting just below him.

Uncle Cross. The comfort of his face and big steps. "Why, there was so much noise down yonder I just had to come on up. Here you go."

A large tin soldier. A redcoat who walked and played the drum.

"For me? For me, Uncle Cross?"

"Came from England. Came special for you."

"It's so pretty."

"Watch now." The magic tap of his thumb. The soldier's head twisted. The sticks moved in his hands. "Rum-ti-tum. Rumti-ti-ti-tum."

"It's not for me. It's too pretty."

"Oh, yes. Your drummer. All yours."

A crash downstairs.

"Why do they do that, Uncle Cross?"

"It's just grown-ups. It's just their way."

"Not on Christmas Eve, though."

"Sometimes."

"You never yell, Uncle Cross."

"Got a weak voice."

"I love you, Uncle Cross."

"You scoot under the covers now."

"I got a redcoat drummer."

"Yes, sir. You do. You surely do."

Memories though. The old Uncle Cross. The boyhood uncle. Be wary of your memories here.

Now his uncle's office waited like barren comb in the

house. The furniture was comfortable and modern. Upon the walls behind his desk hung awards and citations: best dressed and best tailored and the Mr. Dimple award. On the left wall was a full-length picture of Blake's grandmother and Jess. They had necessary eyes and supportive faces. They had touch and see on their lips. Just to the photograph's side hung the largest speckled trout ever caught off the shores of Port Sound. Thirty-one pounds. The dark scales still seemed to shout defiance. The mouth pursed round and open for air. The eyes jumped toward the dark pool of the coal grate. On the right-hand wall lay a large mirror, to its right side a top hat and pair of white gloves. Along the entire remainder of the wall ran a collection of pen-and-ink drawings done by his uncle. The Aztec civilization. Mostly temples and exquisite masonry, but also intricately dressed Aztec chiefs, their faces flawless and chosen. Toward the bottom rank of the fifty or so frames lay a few drawings that detailed blood sacrifices and the removal of hearts.

Glancing into the mirror, Cross sat down on a sofa near the black coal grate and patted a place beside him.

Blake eased next to him, feeling a little relieved by his uncle's smile and the benign signal of his hand. Never sit beside an unsmiling uncle.

"Well," Cross breathed out looking at him warmly. He got up and took his cloisonné cup to a perking coffee pot on the corner of his desk. He filled it, then turned, still smiling, almost as if embarrassed. "I suppose you think your Aunt Millis and I have been needlessly tormenting your mother again."

"I *am* opposed to needless tormenting. Of course, justified tormenting is quite different."

"Your mother's wit. Good," Cross said, nodding.

"Why did you have the Birddogs out again?"

Cross was tipping the end of his finger into his cup and pursing his lips.

"I got the answer," Blake said. "You sent those guys to watch out for her. To protect her from her drunken self."

"She hasn't been drinking much lately," Cross said.

"The pills then. She's threatening her own life, and you're just trying to preserve her from suicide."

"Not at all."

Blake fitted a hand behind his neck and waited. Never commit yourself to their territory so openly.

"Put it together. It's two and two."

"Four," Blake popped off.

"Four and four," Cross said patiently.

"Okay."

"Your mother and her need for security."

"She wants—that is, she needs to be chased all over town. Threatened with incarceration and maybe something worse."

"The men I sent were to watch and follow. Jess needs to know that we—Millis and I—care for her. It's childish. It's a deficiency. Maybe we all suffer from this. I accept it."

"I don't buy all this honesty."

"Your mother needs psychologies other than her own. She will take everyone and pull them into herself."

"But you never do that."

"Sometimes," Cross said, sipping at his coffee.

"Hey! Hello! This is your nephew calling. I know you people here."

"She will never leave with you."

"I see. She's laying a trap, right? Trying to snooker me."

"Jess would never do that to you or to anyone else in this family. She has—great love. We know that here."

"You're damn right you know it. And you want to keep it home every night and on the weekends, don't you?"

"Maybe so. Maybe we're bad people. Intemperate. Malicious."

"Now, I'm not accusing you of being evil," Blake said,

unable to keep himself hard, as usual buckling under any semblance of humility.

"There are some rotten places in me, I know that," Cross said, hands contrite upon his knee.

"Hell, I've got them too," Blake said, losing.

"Just remember once in a while that when you were a kid I tried to help out. I taught you how to tie a double Windsor and not to eat the pope's nose. I made you stop hiding cans of food."

Blake was blocked down and out. He *had* hidden food once. In this house. In this place of abundance, he had stashed cans of food because everyone was so totally embroiled in their glorious fanfare lives that they forgot to feed him.

His uncle had not hired a cook in those days. His mother had her radio show and whatever else. His grandmother was always at her society luncheons and suppers, though she was hardly society. Even his father (obsessed by some new work) never noticed how thin and quiet Blake would become. Blake knew the other boys had meals of chicken and dumplings, ham and roast beef, because they boasted of their splendid meals at recess, their pockets stuffed with treats and homemade candies. Even now Blake could see the other boys as the last school bell rang, piling toward home to overflowing kitchens. His lot had been to walk home through the black frost of the woods sipping a tonic the doctors had given him for ten-year-old nerves. He remembered how his grandmother's stove sat old and recalcitrant as its owner, begrudging even the warmth of its pilot light, the oven and burners mordantly clean. Sometimes he had made faces at the oven, called it names, and once when he was very hungry and out of the tonic, he defiled the main burner with catsup and turned her on high. There was punishment, but he had had his way with the stove.

"I remember your help. You bought me things to eat. I'm not accusing you," Blake said.

"You learned to live by your wits and your guts in a house among people who dealt in surpluses. That is a hard thing to do: to see that you are surrounded by all you need and yet still be needful of all that surrounds you. You learned to see through us clearly, to hold your mother against the light and trace her out." Then he added, "And that's not easy."

"You know, at ten . . ." Blake paused, a little lost now. ". . . At ten, I thought I could see deeper and suffer more than whole battalions of grown-ups. Beyond my years and all."

"You remember when I would bring you boiled shrimp and avocado? We would eat together."

"Those were good times."

"Do you remember the present and the train ride?" Cross asked, his voice silk and currents.

"The fish, too," Blake said.

"The silver fish."

"It was cutting cold. Awful. And we were going on the train to visit mother at the hospital. Inside I was hurting pretty bad. Then you walked into the car carrying the box all wrapped in ribbons and paper. And when I opened it up there was sweet-smelling clay and those earthworms. Red and glistening."

"The train pulled down at Reidsville."

"How did you find that pond? Somehow you did. It appeared. I looked down and saw them. The fish. So silent in the pool."

"How many did you catch?"

"Seven."

"Ah. You have a good memory."

"I set the earthworms on the hook and those ole fish just flew right to me. Like magic. Like gifts."

"Silver and blue."

"You told me they were just for me." Blake spoke very quietly.

"I thought that little boy's heart would break and sink for joy."

"Yeah. Me too. Me too," Blake said, trying to keep the emotion low and bring himself back up. "But tonight you sent those guys out hunting."

"To watch."

"They had guns. That Raphael guy is crazy. Cross, I'm telling you he was going to kill us."

Cross deliberately tapped the butt of a cigarette on his thumbnail. "You know debit collectors. Sometimes they take along guns. The business is rough for them. And you know too that they would never pull one on you."

"What did you tell them to do to us?"

"To bring you here *if* Jess looked in bad shape."

"They did a lot more. Raphael did."

"Blake, I think you've been understudying your mother tonight," Cross said, his eyes free and direct.

Passing into family you had to be most careful and quiet. You strolled through them whistling and not looking to either side. "We ended up in the slaughterhouse, you know?"

"It's been your mother's favorite set since you've been gone. Your father went there, too. My, they did enjoy their scenes late at night."

Blake set his elbows on his knees. He summoned his calmest and most accusing voice. "Mother has implied that Daddy did not die naturally."

"And you think she should not be watched, cared for?"

"For months I've suspected the same thing."

"Your father died of a heart attack," Cross said, running a perfect thumb over his clean jaw.

"See, I don't think so at all. Jess said—"

Cross broke in quickly. "You simply don't want his death to have been an ordinary one. You want—just like Jess—some grand exit. Suicide. A devastating accident."

Blake felt his uncle tuning him in fine now.

"Now, you would probably prefer the idea of suicide, just like Jess," Cross said, his finger rolling around the rim of the cup, bringing a hum from it.

"Just one time you answer me straight," Blake said as the ring of cloisonné grew purer. "How did Daddy die?"

"Simple heart attack," Cross said. He set down his coffee, lit a cigarette, and blew out an unwavering line of smoke.

Blake couldn't read anything else in his uncle's face. He looked in all the familiar places there but saw only this one answer.

"We found your father on the bathroom floor. Alfbender was there. You can ask him. I told Jess compassionately, though directly. Hysterically as the days passed, she convinced herself of a more dramatic end. Alfbender talked to her. Told her Joe was dead natural. But you see suicide sounds so much more tragic. So Greek. Someone could be blamed then. Herself and the family. It is important for her to be in pain."

Cross meticulously poured himself more coffee. One arm folded neatly behind the sofa, fingers holding the cigarette. His shoulder fought off an incipient slouch. "Let Uncle Cross give his favorite nephew a little advice. You clear these notions out of your head now, boy. You learn to live offstage."

He gave Blake the family wink and nod and left the room in smoke and logic.

His uncle's words were always confounding. The reasoning behind them acute. His instinct for truth—jugular. Maybe Cross was exactly right. Maybe his own idea of his father's death bloomed as pure theater and was indicative of his mother's weakness.

He looked at himself closely now. Was he going to be a victim too, just like Mother? Always hunted, always eaten up by others? He felt himself wanting to study the proposal. To sit back and daydream of what he would be like in twenty years. A Valium addict maybe? His mother dead or incarcerated and the silver-haired Cross and arthritic Millis chasing *him* all over town?

Blake stood up. Take a walk now. Get away from the house and these thoughts.

Outside, in the unmistakable air, he had always done better thinking. Some distance away from the house he sat down by a band of bulrushes. Smelling of late pollen and the salt from the sea, the ground felt wet. In the distance a ship's horn sounded. Blake took a couple of ampicillins from his match box and swallowed. How many had he taken tonight?

In a moment, Blake stood up and walked slowly toward the black lowland woods and stopped at the edge. Startled by something in the dark, a white crane flushed into a clearing of trees and cried out at a prowling below that Blake could not see. He tensed as he remembered the scream.

Sharply, from out of the dark, just by the edge of the woods, whistled a high long note. A bird? Or the wind perhaps? Again the sound rose and, light as a shadow and as silent, Alfbender emerged into the open, piccolo at his lips.

"Miss me?" Alfbender asked.

"Damn," Blake answered. "You startled hell out of me."

"Had to get a bath. Get my wrists taped up."

"Why did you leave us like that?"

"I'm sorry. I got scared. Really scared."

"Do you know what happened?"

"Yeah. I do."

"How?"

"I asked some questions. Found Thaggart in the hospital. Blake, I'm really sorry I ran. I got no guts."

"What happened to Thaggart?"

"Raphael knifed him."

"Raphael," Blake said to himself.

"We could call the cops but Raphael's too good at the shadows. He'd smell the badges coming. He's hunting, Blake. There ain't no doubt. He's after Jess."

Blake looked about him through the trees. The Halloween moon was low upon the sea. The air was suddenly cooler.

"What time you got?"

Alfbender looked at his watch. "Close to one-thirty."

"The best plan is still to get her out of town. We just watch careful. In daylight, when she's gone, we can get Raphael. We've got to. He'd follow her. Right now she's safe in the house," Blake said.

"You think so?"

"Don't you?"

"Nope." Alfbender rubbed the piccolo behind his ear. "You go on inside. Lock up good. I'll hang out here around the window ledges. I don't think Thaggart saw Raphael's move. We got to watch close."

"We'll be alright. We'll be moving again soon," Blake said. He went back into the house.

When Blake entered the card room, Cross and Jess were sitting at the parqueted card table. Blake knew they were aware of him, but they said nothing and continued their game. This room was the smallest of the house. It had a double door at the far end and no windows. But upon the walls from ceiling to floor hung hundreds of butterflies, so that all four walls shimmered in color. His grandmother's collection. How appropriate, thought Blake.

When Blake sat on the sofa, his uncle turned, offering a smile. His suit coat removed, Cross sat in his creaseless white shirt, sipping his coffee. Jess's eyes never left the shuffling of the cards. Her face was flushed now, a little swollen from the whiskey. Violence fluttered in the cards.

"Three-card draw. Nothing wild," Cross said, shuffling.

Jess leveled her face. A baiting grin revealed her yellowing teeth. Her eyes seemed tired. Whiskey glamour. "Nothing for chance?" she asked.

"We're all by ourselves."

"Nothing outside to hope for? Nothing out of the great blue to save us?"

"Come on, sister."

"Pretty," Jess said looking diagnostically at Cross's face, his hair.

"I am not dyeing my hair," Cross said, catching her eyes.

"Now—you are not."

"I only tinted it before."

"You never hinted that you tinted."

"You would hurt me, I thought."

"Because of what?"

"My vanity. I thought I had hidden it pretty well from you." Cross was in control.

"You have always kept four mirrors in your room."

"Not large mirrors, though."

"No."

"And they aren't busily cluttered together. Different walls. Different corners—"

"Different angles."

"You knew all the while."

Jess put down her cards, rolled her eyes toward a collection of monarchs. "I remember the first time I ever peeked and saw you work out with your silly barbells."

"You never peeked!" Cross said mockingly.

"It was rather late at night. You had taken the two candelabra from the dining-room table and put them beside your standing mirror. There you were—sixteen, stripped naked, glistening in cooking oil. Holding a dumbbell in one hand and one of Mother's leather belts in the other. The tall mirror was before you. The smaller ones were positioned at just the right points to catch every flicker of muscle. Then you hoisted up the dumbbell and popped the belt and mumbled something like: 'On your faces! On your faces! Let no one behold the countenance of the divinity!' "

"Oh my," Cross said, looking somewhat off balance.

Blake snickered.

"I was execrable."

"You were cute," Jess said, love now on her face.

"Well, I don't do such things anymore."

"You still have the mirrors."

Cross tugged at his ear. "I seem to have lost Mother's belt."

"So now you merely shave your face and knot your tie and give yourself a manly slap on the chin."

"Well, once in a while I take a little turn around."

"Just a wee one."

"Very brisk."

"And not at all in excess," Jess said, squaring her chin, while she took a swallow of her drink.

Cross pinched his nose and grinned. "Somehow I feel that if I keep things very orderly, very—handsome in my face and body, I am alright."

"I have the same thoughts."

"I still have in my mind what we did as children. Standing by the garden pools. Watching ourselves in the currents of the water."

"You grew very upset with the crayfish."

"They moved down there. I like my images still."

Jess nodded her head in mock support.

"We painted faces on one another. Whole days, weeks lost to mud faces and costumes by the garden pools. I was happy," Cross said.

"They *were* pretty faces. Happy charades."

"And we were beautiful children. Mother used to say the wind whistled at us from the chimney tops."

"We played monsters too," Jess said.

"Seldom really."

"Even on bright sunny days we played beasts. Ghouls chasing one another in the woods."

Cross changed course. "Millis has talked of having a face lift, you know?"

"Oh? She's found a contractor?"

"Now, now. You must do something to keep all the girlishness in your face."

Jess's eyes gathered themselves. "Yes. A morning routine. On the stool generally. I pinch my titties and gurgle over bare-chested young men in the Sears underwear ads."

"Jessica!" Cross tugged his clean cuffs. "*I* do pushups. Shoot a few hoops."

"Sports! I love the youthfulness of it all. Young men and baseball bats. I've always had a penchant for both."

Cross reshuffled the cards. "How many?"

"I'm planning to dump two," Jess said quaintly.

"Better check your hand, maybe."

"They're low cards. They pull me down."

"You've always gone down far too easily. Far too often."

"I take my little falls graciously."

"Joyfully. Up and down. All about town," Cross recited.

Jess wove her fingers together and closed them into her palms. "At least when my mother cried out I had the guts to go to her. I sat beside her dying body and gave some comfort."

Blake could see tension hemming up Cross's eyes. His uncle dealt out two cards apiece.

"I wonder how many times I did hear her cry out in the night?" Jess asked.

"Your room was closer," Cross said in a controlled voice.

"Bad lungs, remember? Emphysema. She would start coughing, then become frightened and couldn't breathe. She used to call out: 'Cross! Oh, Cross, come here!' "

"That happened only once."

"Many, many times in the cold night."

"I came. I was there."

"*Once* you were there. God knows how many drinks it took you to answer her. You wormed into the room. There she was—covered in the vomit of supper, lungs as loose as custard."

"I held her hand and we said a prayer together."

"You stood there gagging like a new nurse."

123

"I just had never seen anything like that, Jessica."

"She was gasping. She said: 'The mask. The mask.' And pointed toward the oxygen rig. You cowered against the wall."

"Damn it! I got her the mask. I went right over to her."

"So you shook your way across the room, picked up the apparatus, and then just stood there. Horrified."

"She was cursing. I never saw her like that. I never heard those kinds of words from her."

"Yes, she was cursing. Let's see, what was it like." Jess leaned powerfully toward Cross. " 'Damn you . . . damn you . . . you weak—you weak little—' And she fell back, sputum rolling out her poor old mouth. Turning blue. Needing you, Cross. Needing you to help her breathe. Your mother begging you for life, for air."

"Stop it now!"

"You did get the mask finally. Her hands ripped at your cuffs. You shook. You trembled. Then when she just managed to get her first air, your hand brushed her chest, the vomit there, and you jumped back."

"You weren't there!"

"I saw it all from just outside her door. I saw my big brave brother go to his knees. Sobbing and wretching. Wretching and sobbing while his mother bubbled for air like a carp. If I hadn't come in she would never have seen the morning."

Cross sat back in his chair. He took a handkerchief from his back pocket and dabbed at the corners of his mouth.

Jess had blotches of color across her cheeks. She caught up a gin bottle from under the chair.

"Bet," Cross said.

"Two chips."

"See and raise four."

"See and raise two more."

"Four more."

"I can go on as long as you can."

"We'll see. Call."

Genteelly, Jess laid down her hand. "Too tough for you, I think."

"No," Cross said.

"Let's see them then."

"Three of a kind."

"Doesn't beat a flush."

"Does."

"Doesn't."

"Does."

"Doesn't."

Silly words now. Cross was resting. Jess was allowing him. Blake could see it.

Cross lit a cigarette and inhaled. He shuffled the cards again and control slowly came back to his face. Now all his movements changed to two-quarter time. Slow and casual, his eyes and mouth concerned, his cheeks still.

"Ole Joe was pretty good at cards."

"Dealing in Las Vegas was one of his more romantic lies."

"If you had strolled with him instead of racing against him—if you had encouraged him he could have been a better man. He had a genius and was prolific."

"He was crafty and a Catholic."

"You denied him, Jess."

"And more than three times, or this spotless homestead would be overrun with buck-toothed window-breakers."

"He called out to *you* many times in the night."

"Yes. He did."

"You were always across town with some silky-eyed boy."

"Not always. Sometimes we shot crap in the downstairs bathtub. Nude, crude, and criminally clean." Jess put a finger to her lips. "What a perfectly delightful line. Did you take that down, Buckles?"

"I remember the night you discovered you were about to have a baby."

Jess's fingers tightened around the bottle. "Now, Cross," she said.

"Joe was very proud."

"Yes. He was shining. Oh, yes, that night he flashed pure as an altar."

"You said something cruel. Very cruel," Cross said.

"I was young. I was heavy."

" 'You've ruined me,' I think you said. 'They'll have to crack my hips, open up my belly.' "

"You shouldn't hurt me so for those words, Cross. I didn't know what a baby would do," she said, looking at Blake.

" 'Cut the thing out,' you said."

"Not like that."

" 'Joseph, I want this thing cut out of me or I'll rip it out myself!' "

"No, I was not so coarse! Never horrible and common. I was frightened of what I felt ticking in me. Beneath the fear, I was proud. I became proud." Jess again glanced at Blake. "I didn't know about little babies. Buckles, my mama only told me about the pain and I saw the other fat ladies. They looked so ugly and sad. They didn't wear makeup and they smelled funny. I wanted you, Buckles, and I was proud. But I didn't know it then. You were something growing in me I couldn't see. Like a tumor. Something in there which I didn't have anything to do with and I was so afraid you were going to hurt me. I was afraid you would eat me up and I would not be lovely anymore."

She hid her face. Her mouth was grimacing behind her hands and her neck pulled taut.

Quickly Blake moved beside his mother and got his arms around her, rocking her in the chair. Cross watched them quietly, his broad face secure. Blake felt weak and embarrassed before his uncle. Gutless. "Let's just call it off here," he said. "She's tired. The booze and all."

Cross carefully reached for his many-colored cup as he left

the table. His voice was deference itself. "You stay right by her now. Things are said sometimes. Bad exchanges go on. Try to get the bottle away. It's not good to see her so. I won't have her treating herself so."

His uncle left the room in a conqueror's gait.

Blake laid his head against her cheek for a moment, then sat down in a chair beside her, holding her hands, gazing into the bowl of oranges and flowers upon the sideboard.

Jess sniffed lightly and wrinkled her nose. She loosened her hands from his, rubbed at her eyes, and came out smiling. "You know, early in the going I thought I had him. There was a little giving there. I could feel it."

"He uses his senses like a knife. He knows exactly how deeply to cut."

"We all have our gifts."

"You could have broken him. You should have pressed harder."

"He hurt you, didn't he?"

"I don't care."

Jess reached over and stroked his hair. "Are you upset because of what Cross said?"

Beyond the liquor and the lateness of the hour Blake saw feeling for him in her eyes. "I'm alright. But you gave up. You let him take you."

"He's losing me, he thinks. So I gave him something. A card-table victory. Nothing more."

"That's good. That's fine," Blake said. "As long as you're cutting the lines. As long as he understands you're finished here. Leaving."

Jess placed one of her thumbs under his left eye and one under her own. She pulled down on the soft flesh. "What do you see?"

"An old, gouty-looking eyeball," Blake said.

"Come on now. Don't scold Mother's complexion."

127

"Damned ole thing looks like it's running pure gin," Blake said, grinning.

Jess pushed down a little harder on his cheek, trying not to smile. "Yours looks like a distress message from a thirty-pound pigeon."

They both pulled away and laughed. Jess kissed her thumb and planted it on his nose. "I wanted you to see some determination there. I realize you have to look in between the Gordon's capillary system, but it's there, Buckles. I'm trying to let them know very gently. They have investments in me and they're hurting now. There's no need to sow salt in them. You have to respect wounds. You just do."

Blake nodded. Mothers spoke in lullabies.

"Let's take a gander at the stars," Jess said freshly. She relit her cigar and went out the double doors onto the balcony.

Standing by the railing she caught a few puffs, then tossed the cigar away. Blake thought suddenly of Raphael and moved beside her.

Jess sighed and sat down against the flank of the house and pulled Blake alongside. He had just closed his eyes when he felt something cool against his cheek. Jess held an orange out to him. He peeled the fruit and divided it between them.

"A little vitamin C to keep us fit," Jess said.

"Oranges by the starlight," Blake said.

"Mother knows about pick-me-ups."

"I feel like grumbling and saying no."

"We have to keep our strength."

"We are winning, aren't we?" Blake asked.

"Down to the last sweet wedge, we are running away with it."

Blake matched his palms to hers. "You know, sometimes I just find myself remembering little rules you used to recite me." Her head laid against him. "When you said, 'Alright, son, straighten those shoulders. Don't slouch or you'll look like an old man.' Even something that small, that silly turned out to be true. Why, Mama, I see friends of mine now who look almost swaybacked. Pot bellies and crooked spines. They look thirty years old."

"Ancient, Buckles, ancient. Probably feel it."

"But they're all true. All those little warnings you used to give."

"I must have missed once in a while."

"When you absolutely ordered me to say *sir* and *ma'am* I detested it. But I made a habit of the politeness, and now when I say *sir* to some fellow—yes, sir, or thank you, ma'am —their faces break my way every time."

"Makes them feel respected. Makes them feel more—loved, I guess."

"You know one of the best things you taught me?"

Jess rubbed his hands. He could feel the stickiness of the orange.

"Well, it wasn't to stop popping your knuckles. Look at those ugly things. On such aristocratic hands, too."

Jess loved the "aristocratic" role: for herself, for Blake, her family. Blake gripped her about the waist. "You said go to the still place inside of you. When things start exploding, when you hurt pretty bad, go to the quiet place and listen to the voice and be still."

"I had it once. A long time back. There was that place in me, too. Maybe I passed it down your way too soon."

"You still have it."

"Yeah, through the evening we've seen my marvelous control. My stunning aplomb in matters of distress. Retreating into myself is like sending a hen to roost with the foxes: hackles and horror."

"The stillness is hope in us, I think. Part of something else out there. Something that lasts. You think maybe that's so?"

"I don't know. You could kick it around and see."

"Matches, matches. Who's got the matches?" Blake whispered close to her ear.

Jess laughed, rubbed her knuckles into her eyes, then whispered back. "The wee boy. The wee boy. The wee boy with the pie."

"Peach pie. Sweet pie. Why'd he make the deep pie?"

"To cook it for his mama so she would never die," Jess said.

They seemed extraordinarily close for a time.

"Say, did I ever straight out tell you that you are beautiful?" Jess asked, her voice round in its warmth.

"Oh, Mama."

"Well then . . ." She raised up and put her nose crinkly against his. "You are a prince, Mr. Pasque." She kissed him.

"A mother's eyes," Blake said.

"Listen, kid, I got the stage's eyes. You're a knockout. When you walk down the street you got the form. A radiance."

"Don't go on now, Mama."

"When you get low, just look in the mirror and say—that's snappy stuff there."

"It just doesn't stay with me. No comfort."

"It's better than those internal safaris searching for the truth oil. That's for kids. 'When I became a man I put away childish things.' It's better to go for something solid, something rare and desired. Do you know there are thousands, millions of people who would swear anything, deny more, and bargain off years of their life to be like us? So pretty. We have that gift at least in this house. Down to spades we've got those pretty angles."

They finished the orange and sucked their fingers. Jess lay in his arms smelling of fruit and the bare fineness of her ambergris. The odor of whiskey was with her too and the sadness of it, of anything that bound her. So now in the very, very quiet of the late moon's setting, curved as the wheaten edge of his mother's lashes, Blake sat somewhere between joy and despair. For to have your mother ill and in your arms consumed by unchallengeable disease went past misery. But if you held her with the hope that she had really taken the first step toward reality, she seemed to you pure and radiant.

"Raphael," Blake said.

"Not here," Jess said.

"Alfbender told me he cut up Thaggart."

"The barrister is prone to bend a tale."

"No, this was the truth."

"I'll bet."

"Alfbender said Raphael is after you. He's right. Sticking Thaggart wasn't trick or treat, Jess. Don't you see that?"

"Nope," Jess said sitting up, assuming the lotus. She bent at the waist, stretched, exhaled. "Just a wee bit of paranoia creeping in there."

"Not with Raphael. Not with him," Blake said. "Besides, I just got over one spell of paranoia. Cross pretty well convinced me that Daddy died natural." Then he caught himself. He hadn't meant to be provocative. But it was *his* freedom, too.

Jess moved farther out onto the balcony. "Feel all better about it?"

What's the point in throwing your mother's lie in her own face.

"I'm just saying I had my crazy notions, too. I was sure something else had happened. I even thought he might have committed suicide or been murdered."

"Murder's not bad," Jess said.

A little dig now. "I wonder why we always have to have the spectacular crutch."

"A beastie cut him down in the night, huh?"

"It was in the back of my mind," Blake said.

"The beast took him. Some night-filled thing." Jess's eyes wove over. She began to make up the story. "There's no way to trail the thing down now. We'll never find the last eyes which looked into his."

"Maybe he fought, though," Blake said, giving in to her. Letting her play. "Maybe he got in a good lick."

"He cracked his jaw. He made the beast just hurt bad. Then he laughed like music," Jess said.

"Oh, I know he did. He taunted what had him. He kissed its nose and crushed its brain."

"When the thing hit him he didn't really feel anything, and if he did, maybe he just cursed and swung again. He went down cursing and laughing."

"Those blue eyes sang," Blake said. "They went down singing in blood."

"They were laughing eyes. They were winning."

"If we could just have read his eyes we could have seen the face that put him on the ground so low."

Jess laid her fingers against her deep temples and the lined muscles of her cheeks. "I wanted to follow the beast, Buckles. I wanted to hunt him down."

"Too hard."

"But I can't. I'm impotent. Women are impotent, aren't they?"

"No use in hunting the dark," Blake said.

"Something rabid in the dark."

"It's changed probably. To go after it would be tracking the air."

"No, it's the same, I really think. Out there clattering its paws and looking for some other pulse."

"Hey." Blake shook her foot. "This is just playacting. Let's not go too deep now."

"But what if it were real? What if your father had been murdered? See, you forget these things."

"Well, then maybe I'd just hate the beast. Knowing myself, I'd probably just hate him and be afraid of him in the dark. I wouldn't go after him, though. I'm not a hunter."

"Oh, Buckles, you've got stone in your guts," Jess said laying her fingers on his lips. "If there is any truth to this thing you can hunt the murderer down. I know that, honey."

"I just don't think I could is all."

"Your heart's big. You can do bunches of revenge."

"Why?"

"Dear God." Jess closed her eyes.

"You see, you people are different from me. I know you're all tough."

"Just think of whatever it was that killed your father."

Blake could feel the fever in his eyes. He had made a mistake by going this far with the story.

"I'll tell you this. I could track this beast and slit his throat and gut him like a rabid dog. I could rinse my hands in his oily guts and never catch a breath."

"I think you could."

Jess slid over next to him and drew a finger down his nose. "Same nose. Same fine eyes as Mother. Same will. Tell me now you could do it."

"I love you, Mama. That's what I'll tell you. I love you."

"You can hate, too. Now just tell me how you could chew this creature's eyes up and spit them out."

Get away from this. Get out of her story now. "There's no creature."

"Damn you," Jess said very quietly.

"Don't tease me, Mama."

"Damn this innocence. This appalling negligence in you."

"You know, some things you say I don't forget."

"Weakling."

"Okay."

"Your heart would drain through a sieve."

"Look. There's nothing to do," Blake said and got up. He felt dizzy. Spots cruised in his eyes.

Just when they were clearing, he felt a shock, a sting across his face. He fell back a few steps.

"Did you feel that? Is there something to do now?"

Blake drew back against the house. Tried to get some sense rolling.

"Don't hit back because it's Mother now. Be kind. Be sweet. You'll drown in milk and honey."

Again she slapped him. Water rushed into his mouth. He raised his hands up to his face.

"Something? You must feel something strong in you. Think about your father. Somebody did this to him. Only bashed his brains out. Strike back. Damn you! Damn!" She caught his hand and raised it toward her face.

Millis appeared at the door carrying a tray.

"Alright, alright. Let's stop this right now." She placed a drink into Blake's hand. His eyes and face were burning. He didn't look at his mother.

Millis handed Jess a drink. "Now, just settle ourselves down here. Sip something cool and try to think pleasantly."

"He's a fish," Jess said, a dry smile at her lips. "Look at those eyes."

Blake was shaking.

"Look at him," Jess said. "He just won't boil."

Millis was all slushy words and fluttering hands.

"Buckles, you go out to the front porch now. Yes indeed. Uh-huh, you drink your toddy and have a walk for yourself, yes. I'll be here. Go on straight now. Never you mind."

Blake moved backwards through the door. His mother's face was crippling. He had seen the expression before. He had hoped that it was not a real part of her.

"You know—I bet—he's even got a little, tiny, milk-white dick," Jess said.

Blake set down his drink and turned his back.

"How big do you swing, son? What do you carry on you down there? Goodness and light?"

Blake stood on the front porch. Well, damn her to hell! Damn all of them! You couldn't be easygoing. You couldn't play with them at all or they snapped you up. He kicked a flower pot into the front yard.

Alfbender moseyed out of the dark. "They must have salted you down pretty good." He had knotted his hair into one long braid which lay on the top of his shoulder.

"I don't have to go through all this shit."

"They're rough folks, alright."

"I can be rough too. The hell with them. Let them go ahead and play their damn games. I'm sick of it. I hate them all."

Alfbender sat down in a rocker beneath the brown shade of the porch light. "How much do you hate them?"

"Enough to break somebody's ass. I'm telling you, Alf, one day Mama's going to say something not half as bad as just now and I'll slap the shit out of her. She thinks I don't have the guts. Damn, where are her eyes!"

"Her eyes are just as sharp as ever. Look what she's done."

"She ain't done nothing."

"Got you pretty steamed up."

"She slapped me. Right in the face. She hit hard, too."

"Did you poke her back?"

"I'm telling you I could do that."

"Did you?"

"Listen, if I started on her maybe I'd do a lot more."

"Good. She needs it. A couple pokes in the snoot might cool her down. You ought to try it."

Blake stared at the lawyer. He took a breath and sunk his hands in his pockets, then sat in a wicker chair beside Alf-bender.

Thin fall bugs batted the porch light. The wicker chair tittered as the wind was picking up out of the southwest. The smell of the sulfurous marsh was warm and heavy.

Alfbender put the tip of his braid to his nose.

"What the hell did you do that for?" Blake asked.

"Comfortable."

"You look ridiculous."

"You got some fever?"

"Yeah, I got some fever."

"You seen ole Munson?"

"Maybe he had the good sense to run off. Maybe I'll do the same thing."

"Can't."

"The hell I can't."

"We got our friend Raphael to worry about."

Blake's face was still stinging.

"You should just stay in the house. He's too creepy. I'm afraid of him coming in some way I can't see. You should stay right in there."

"Do you really think this guy would try to break into a houseful of people?"

"He's just that crazy."

"He's off in a bar drinking. I'm not worried about him. It's my family that bothers me. I'm going for a swim."

"Go on, freeze your ass," Alfbender said. Then, more quietly. "Blake, you be careful in the dark."

Blake went down the steps, turned. "Who you trying to scare, Alf? What kind of game are *you* playing?"

Alfbender raised his hands in silent defense.

Blake went across the yard and into a stretch of woods. He needed to get away from them. He needed not to think for a while. Why worry about Raphael. Crazy or not, his job was done when Cross opened the door to them.

He was stepping down through a bank of briers just before the beach when he heard a noise. He stopped. The moon sent light through the pines. He used his eyes fast now, searching everything near him. Rotted logs. Stumps. Twisted saplings. He listened and heard only the sound of the woods: leaves and dry branches in the wind, the scuttle of beetles. Nothing was in the woods. Nothing was waiting. Alfbender had just spooked him. Simple as that. He took a couple of deliberate steps and waited. Fine. No shadows. Just fine. He made his way through the briers and down to the level beach. He looked around him again. To the left the beach was clear all the way to the darkness of the great marsh. The lights of Port Sound glowed beyond and over it. His right side was open sand. You're okay now. You're fine.

Blake stripped off his clothes. The stars seemed hard, like blue-white thorns pressed against the moon. The buoys flashed out green light, and their bells clanged sharp and alone to the rocks and the last of the land. The water rushed his calves. His tits drew up hard. He got three deep breaths, then thought of going back. The water was cold, but he felt the muscles of his legs loosening now, and the rest of his body demanded the cold. The shock might get him through until seven. Until the train.

He dove in and felt the blood start across the surface of his skin. Every muscle sprang tight and complained. Automatically he sucked in new air and kicked into the crawl. He swam a few feet, but his breath wasn't any good and he felt dizzy. He switched to a sidestroke and then felt sand. Twenty feet away the back of a sandbar rose from the surface. This side of the island had no waves and he came up on the bar quickly. He laid in the shallows of the sandbar. The water here was warmer. He could feel his muscles un-hitching.

As usual Alfbender was right. Jess had gotten out of him exactly what she needed. She'd led him down the same old path. Sniped him right in the gut. When would he pick up the clues? When would he learn to just stay clear? Blake laughed at himself now. There he stood, having his face battered in. At least you could have blocked, dummy. You could have shuffled around a bit and snorted. He felt his forehead: cool. Maybe he had broken the fever. He slid back down into deeper water. Maybe next time he would let Jess hold one on the nose. Bap, right on the snoot. He smiled and backstroked to shore. He felt weak now, but he was laughing. You got to put some distance on them with a little humor, he thought.

Blake was shaking sand from his shoes in the side yard when he saw something moving toward the house. The form opened the back bathroom window and leaped belly first to the ledge. Alfbender for sure. But he appeared to have changed clothes. He seemed to be mostly in white now. He dissolved quickly into the dark of the room. Blake was amused. Alfbender never thought of using regular doors or even regular windows. There always had to be a clever way of entering. He was probably going to the kitchen for chicken in the refrigerator. All the lights were out in the back of the house, and Blake recalled how Alfbender loved to steal food and eat in the dark.

On the edge of the front lawn the pampas grass was humming in the early-morning wind. Had to be nearly three o'clock, Blake thought. He sat down in the very heart of the grass to put on his shoes. From here he could see the large front room of his home. The windows were clear light. His whole family was standing there. Apparently they had reached some small respite now. Maybe Jess could leave without more gunplay. Cross was laughing and Jess curtsied. Even from here they seemed so artful, their faces and their motions strong and enticing, utterly graceful. Blake was going down so easily into the very heart of them. Why was it?

Out of the side library window Alfbender silently dropped to the ground. The lawyer paused, then quietly in a strange movement he stepped toward the front of the house. He had a small sack over his shoulder and was carrying something that looked like a bucket. He eased toward the front steps and knelt down. Blake tugged on his shoes. Alfbender appeared to be painting. Slipping into the house seemed very much like the lawyer, but coming out again so soon puzzled Blake. Now he was using white paint and Blake was trying to construct the first word.

A rap on the side of his face. Blake jumped and lost his

balance. Alfbender had his fingers at his lips. He knelt down beside Blake, holding the pistol across his knee.

"He's got the whole place painted up like that," Alfbender said.

Raphael.

Blake felt his heart missing beats. He held his breath, staring at the lawyer, letting his heart slow down. He turned on an elbow and looked toward the white figure on the front steps. "I thought it was you."

"Not naked, my friend. Not buck naked, thank you, sir."

Blake squinted. As the figure moved and passed into more light, Blake saw that Raphael was nude. The lettering was going faster now.

"He's been here a good ten minutes. Sneaking in and out of the house. Quiet, this one. But so white in the dark."

"What the hell are you doing, then?"

"Watching him. Never far behind."

Blake pushed himself up, ready to move for the house.

"Nope," Alfbender said.

"For Christ's sake. He's out to kill her."

"Not until he finishes his fun."

Blake moved again and Alfbender shoved him down.

Raphael stopped. His head went back and into the air as if he were looking at the stars. Twisting from his waist, he turned around. His blond hair scattered about his neck. Still he held his head very high. His mouth hung low and open.

Blake did not blink his eyes. Alfbender had stopped breathing.

Head thrown back, eyes wide and still, Raphael's face put itself inquisitively at an angle. His open jaws just barely twisted toward where Blake and Alfbender were sitting.

Blake felt seen. He thought of closing his eyes. He knew that Raphael had picked them out.

For a few moments, Raphael's face held directly to the pampas grass. Then the body came back around to the steps and the face and head finally tracked around as well. Raphael painted again.

Alfbender was whispering into his ear. "I've never seen anyone use his body like this guy. He can feel movement around him. And you see the way he lifts his head up? Smelling, I think. Maybe I'm wrong, but following the scent, I'm almost sure."

"How long do we wait?"

"Let him get all involved again. There's no way to get close otherwise. If we wait 'til he forgets the noise, then maybe we got him."

Raphael painted a little longer. He set the bucket down and moved back. Now Blake could read the words: "Jess and Raphael sitting in a tree k-i-s-s-i-n-g—First comes love, then comes marriage. Here comes Jess with her head in a carriage."

"He's got stuff like that all over the house. I looked in the kitchen window with a flashlight. The back of the door reads: 'I was here. Watching. I heard you all laughing!' He wasn't six feet from them."

"You should have caught him."

"I see."

"Damn it. You should have cornered him."

Blake felt the butt of a pistol slap his thigh.

"Here you go."

"Get it off."

"Do something, big man."

Raphael was reaching into the bag about his shoulders. He took something out and then got down on his belly and crawled to one of the two bay windows.

Blake took the pistol. He was surprised at its weight. "I'm getting closer."

Alfbender tapped him on the neck and pointed out to sea. A ship all lights and silence was moving toward the channel.

"Wait on her. She'll sound two longs and a short. Move on the longs. Cover your noise."

Raphael laid on his side beneath one of the windows. He was taking something out of the bag. He did not seem hurried. His hands and arms looked confident: a workman doing his job.

"What's he doing up there?" Blake asked.

"You take a look." From one of his coat pockets Alfbender handed over a small pair of binoculars.

"Amazing," Blake said, glancing at the lawyer, then putting the lenses to his eyes.

Before the light of the windows Raphael's body seemed hard and cut with a body builder's angles. The torso had all its muscles high, taut against the skin. The thighs and calves had been worked on.

The ship neared the mouth of the channel.

They eased up and crouched on their feet. Alfbender pointed to a stack of wood twenty feet to the left of Raphael. The horn blew out of the night, clearly across the sea and beach. They ran quietly on the balls of their feet and sunk down behind the woodpile. For a few breaths they waited. Alfbender poked Blake. He pointed to the lower rank of the woodpile. Blake crept closer, then jerked back.

The large, yellow head of his uncle's dog. Munson's throat had been raggedly slashed. The red bone of the neck protruded. Black blood dried on the logs. The paws had been neatly tucked up into the throat.

Blake dug his knuckles into the dirt and steadied. Alfbender looked at him expressionless. Blake glanced up toward the porch.

Raphael pulled a small jar and spoon from his bag. He began to eat something.

Blake switched his attention to his family. Jess was sitting on the floor, her back to the windows and face upon her knees. Millis was apparently singing and clapping her hands.

Her red-rimmed glasses danced about her neck. Cross was tucking at the handkerchief in his suit pocket. Suddenly Raphael jumped against the wall. Jess had approached the window.

A small flash of light to the left and below. Raphael was holding something shiny in his hands. A knife?

Blake knew Jess had to have seen Raphael. Then he became aware that she was not looking outside. She was primping at her hair. She brushed her hands across her high cheekbones and below her eyes. Dabbing at her lashes, she moved back across the room.

"Time to move," Alfbender said.

Blake looked over his shoulder. The ship was gliding toward the canal, about to make her final call.

"You stay. I'll try to make the willow," Blake said. He started to hand the gun back, but kept it for now.

The ship's horn cut across the hollow air. Blake ran over some open ground, then dodged under the branches of the willow. This time he was sure he had made noise. Looking through the vines, he saw only a part of Raphael. He feared that Raphael's head had again assumed the high, hunting stare, dislocating itself from the body, gauging the noise. Barely separating the branches, Blake saw Raphael quietly gazing through the windows.

Before Raphael, in the flooding light of the room, Jess lay facing the fireplace. Cross sat near her, his head low, in a confessional attitude. At first Blake thought Raphael was merely crouched and watching them, but then he saw movement. Raphael's shoulders seemed tense and working at something before him. Blake remembered the reflection of light. A gun. He was loading a pistol. But he would have done that earlier.

Slowly Raphael let his head drop backward. His arms were pumping fast and the muscles of his sides twisted in the light. On the window two feet over his head, circles began to gleam and spread. His knees went forward and his neck arched even farther back near the floor of the porch.

Blake opened a clear space in the branches.

The window magnified the moisture, and the first two panes began to spread in a silver running, then the next two below them, and still the circles came until just at Raphael's belly, like a clean hole pressed through the glass, the final issue was gleaming, draining down, catching all the light of the chandelier, turning to red and yellow, the softest gold, and from the center of the window to the floor the glass lay sparkling and wet, alive against the light and the unknowing faces.

Raphael fell all the way back and caught himself silently on his palms. He shook his hair and stretched. Lying back on the porch, he rubbed his hands over his shoulders and chest.

Blake had closed himself back into the willow. He heard the wind going through the higher parts of the tree and the tugboats beckoning the ship. He felt disoriented. His eyes hurt. He looked down at the thirty-eight. Gripping the butt tighter, he came up a bit, felt things around him more. Raphael was still lying on the porch.

"Raphael," he called out.

Even Raphael's blond hair did not move.

"Raphael," Blake said again. He stepped from the willow, the gun behind him.

Rising, his back still turned to Blake, Raphael stroked his face and neck with his hands. In one quick leap he spun up and onto the banister. His body was gleaming. He raised his chin triumphantly, his face smart and curious.

"Right here. All the time," Raphael said.

"You got anything? Have you got a knife?"

Suddenly Raphael opened his white palms.

Blake jerked.

Raphael laughed. "I've been following you. I've been just kissing close all night."

"You're sick. You're screwed up bad," Blake said.

"Sometimes I get real confused."

"What's eating you? What the hell's wrong?"

"Way down deep?"

"Way down."

"Love. I love Jess."

"Yeah."

"I do. My own peculiar kind. Just like everybody else in this family." He drifted forward across the railing.

"Just stay up there now."

Raphael paused, then began creeping down. "I'm just like you. Just like the rest of the family. You look at me close and see, huh?"

Alfbender slipped up from the side. "Can you hold him there?"

"I'm alright," Blake said.

"I'll get the cops," Alfbender said. "Don't let him go. If he gets back into the night he's gone. You're sure you can hold him?"

"Call them," Blake said.

Alfbender ran for the front door.

Raphael kept his eyes on Blake. He stretched his arms behind his neck and popped his knuckles. He crossed his arms along his chest. "You think I'm nuts. I know. I'm ashamed of some of the things I done tonight. Some things were hard on you and Jess. Sometimes they were dirty, distasteful things."

Blake held the pistol out front, as if sighting for a shot. You're alright, he said to himself.

Raphael did not look at the pistol. "I hurt Jess because she had hurted me so bad a while back in the hospital. I scared her. I got after her real good tonight." Casually he began approaching.

Blake waved the barrel to make the point.

"Jess is sweet. She's got a love about her, and you got it too.

I can feel it in you. Look at me. I'm like you and all of them. I'm pretty too."

Blake settled his left hand alongside the cylinder of the pistol to steady it. "You don't know me, Raphael. Just stay there."

"By your mama, I do. Just by being around her. Observing her and her toughness."

"You think I'm scared?"

"You're a hard-ass beneath all the other good things. I told you that. A fella can be good and a hard-ass, too. You're one. I'm kind of one too. But I'm stopping right here because I know you'd shoot me if I got up on you."

Blake found that he could take on Raphael's eyes well. His hand felt dry on the pistol.

"So I'll give you the break. I'm going on now. My body is being chilled. I was foolish playing with no clothes on." Raphael turned his side to Blake and started toward the woods.

"Wait," Blake said.

"Left my clothes under some pine straw."

Blake pointed the pistol at Raphael's head. The blue eyes peered back at him through the sights. "Would you hurt Jess?"

If he could just lure him along to the right place. Just make him stay very close for the knife and the gutting. "I care for her a lot. But sometimes I want to be mean."

"But you intend to cut her up or something. You have that feeling?"

"I might do something. I won't lie. Yeah, I've had feelings. I got some clothes in the woods. You stay with me now."

When Raphael moved, the pistol followed his head. "Now it's awful late. The pumpkins is all burned out and my head doesn't feel so good itself. Maybe I better just slow down."

"I guess so," Blake said.

Raphael folded his arms across his stomach and whistled. "What are you doing now?"

Blake shrugged. His arms were tiring from tension, holding the pistol.

"Come on with me. Just follow me off. I'm freezing and I got to go. You can go ahead and shoot me right down. But it would be easier for you if you just came on. There're things I can tell you. Reasons I can give. I ain't going to be freezing out here. Let me get some clothes. You can go ahead and shoot me now or just come with me."

Carefully Raphael backed toward the first few trees in the yard. He took smooth steps. He held his palms out behind him. Then raising his eyebrows and pursing his lips, he whistled some melody, then grinned wide-toothed. His muscles were white and tense in the moonlight, but he seemed to move magically as if on an unseen layer of air.

Let him get ten feet on you. Just ten feet ahead, Blake said to himself. He followed, afraid to glance at the ground ahead.

The black pine woods opened for Raphael. He moved into them. No tree stood in his way. Somehow he sensed and stepped around brambles. About twenty feet into the woods Raphael stopped and turned. His hands held to the air delicately. His hair gathered the last circling light of the moon.

Blake kept the pistol on Raphael's chest. You can't let him go. You've got to stick close. Just hold on 'til the cops come.

I'm going to lead you into the forest, little boy. I'm going to get you in these woods and lick your salty guts.

Blake could feel the wind across his face. He could smell the sea down to his right.

"Here," Raphael said. "Right here." He pointed at his face.

"So?" Blake said. He laid his left palm under the pistol.

"You needn't answer me so rough. You're awful harsh-sounding with me." He moved at an angle toward Blake.

"You wait now. I can see you."

"That's what I want. I want you to just look at me. I ain't

after nobody. I ain't after you." He put a finger to the side of his left eye. "What color? Come on now. What color you see?"

It was too dark, but Blake answered anyway. "Blue."

"And what color are yours?"

"Green."

"Naw, they're blue. Just like mine. We got the same color eyes. And we got the same kind of face. We could be brothers, you and me."

"Maybe so," Blake said.

"I know so. Listen, I used to lay my head on Jess's neck during those long afternoons. I could hear her heart ticking. Sometimes she sang way low in her throat. That's how I kept sane in the hospital."

"What else did you do there? Did you play games? Cards?"

"Oh, come on, Blake. You're just trying to make me talk 'til those police come. I ain't dumb. I ain't real dumb. But I am cold. Yes sir. I got goose eggs on me."

"Where are your clothes?"

"Presto. Watch this." Raphael stooped down and pulled a pair of jeans from under a log.

"Put them on," Blake said. He wondered how many minutes had passed. Maybe Alfbender was talking to the cops right now.

"I'll tell you what though. I ain't waiting on no cops."

Blake kept still.

"It's not in my blood to wait."

"I think you better."

"Well I'm not."

"I'm a good shot."

Raphael shrieked, then covered his mouth.

"I know something about pistols," Blake said. The laugh jarred him.

"No you don't. In the hospital Jess told me everything about you. Why, I doubt if you ever picked one up before.

But that's alright. You ain't going to shoot me cause I'm not one to get shot. Just take me back home. I done all I wanted to tonight. Just sign me back into the hospital."

Raphael had to be lying. He was planning to lead him along and then run off. Blake saw that. But maybe he could stall him. Stay close to him in the woods. The cops would be here soon. Just be tough.

"Okay," Blake said. "I'll go with you to the hospital. But don't try and run off. I'll be close enough to pop you with this thing."

Raphael swept back his hair and clenched a fist. "Alright! I knew you'd take me back. Cops are rough. I knew you'd try to be decent, specially with your brother."

Blake shuddered.

Raphael grinned and put on his jeans. He moved ahead.

Blake pointed the pistol at the center of Raphael's back.

They made their way down a hill. The ground was soft in leaves. Blake grabbed hold of saplings so as not to slip. Ahead the lights of the state park, closed since Labor Day.

They broke out of the woods into mown grass. Merry-go-rounds and empty swings creaked in the wind. A white-walled pool stood full of water stained yellow by fallen leaves. The shuttered concession stand and stacked picnic tables. Beyond lay swinging hand bridges which led to the wooden pavilion in the midst of the great marsh. Blake could feel his heart beating down in his belly.

Raphael turned, hands riding his hips. *Where will I get you now? On the bridges? That'd be nice. I could hang you upside down. Maybe in the pavilion, though. I could handle your spleen in the light.*

You have to keep him out of the marsh, Blake thought. He wants to get down there. You'll lose him. He'll go back after Jess. Blake looked out at the lighted pavilion. If he could get Raphael out on the bridges he could use up time. Once in the pavilion he'd tell him to lie down. Once he had him in light. Alfbender would surely come before then though.

148

"I used to come out here when I was a kid," Blake said.

"Me too," said Raphael. He crossed one bare foot over the other. Put his hands into his back pockets.

"Mother went crazy out here one time," Blake said, keeping his eyes right on Raphael. "She got drunk and stripped off all her clothes and whirled around on the merry-go-round right there."

Raphael looked at the merry-go-round. "You want to do it? You want to spin around? I like doing things like that."

To make him dizzy, Blake knew. "Not now."

"See, I don't need to be on pills. I'm just natural crazy. Organically crazy. It's better to just lock me up and come visit. Don't get too close to the bars either. I might bite. I done worse things. No kidding. I'm the beast. *Le bête.*"

Suddenly Raphael whirled. Blake dropped back. Raphael crept toward the picnic tables. His right hand snapped into the air. "I got him. Look here."

When Raphael opened his palm Blake expected to see nothing. Instead, an orange-and-black monarch butterfly struggled to free itself.

"Ain't he pretty?"

"He's nice," Blake said, his mouth very dry.

"You see them in the fall mostly. I love them. The little things. Little life is best life." He opened his hand. The butterfly flew into the dark.

"If you like these pretty things, then why do you cut them up?"

Blood rose in Raphael's face. He turned toward the hand bridges behind him. "You're mean to say that to me. I was aware of your thinking that about me. I knew you knew. It's something I got wrong with me, like being crippled, and I don't think you should make fun of it. It wasn't just tomfoolishness, you know. I'm sick. You shouldn't point at the sick ones. You shouldn't make fun."

Blake began to approach him, then stopped.

When Raphael turned back around his face was clean and

smiling. "When you was a little boy, what'd you use to do out here?"

Keep him going, Blake thought. "Well, I used to pick plums over there. I'd get me a bucket of red plums and eat them out in the pavilion."

"You mean muscadines?"

"Them big ole red plums that grow way up on the hill."

"Blood plums is what you're talking about," Raphael said and squatted down. Blake did the same.

"I used to stick them," Blake said.

Raphael slid his jaw to one side. "Shit." He kept pace with Blake's eyes. "Using what?"

"Jess's hat pins."

Raphael's face burst open. "Your mama's hat pins?"

"Stuck them through and through. Ole red wood plums."

"Her fine hat pins?"

"Some of Grandma's too."

"Wahoo!" Raphael yelled. The scream cut through the night.

"I just loved it," said Blake quickly in its wake.

"See, we ain't so different. Sassy damn wood plums. Sitting up on their scruffy old tree. They deserved it."

"How'd you like a whole bowlful right now? Red wood plums. Full of summer and sass," Blake said.

"We could just go at it." *Tick, tick.*

"Get us all the fancy hat pins we could."

"Has Jess still got some?"

"Lots," Blake said.

"We could get us big bowls of plums." *Tick, tick.*

"Tons."

"Thousands."

"Hundreds of thousands."

"And those fancy pins." *Tick, tick. Hear your clock running out, sweet boy?*

"With the feathers."

150

"Wouldn't it be pretty," Raphael said.

"We could go out and sit in the pavilion. I like to be way out in the marsh."

"Let's go then," Blake said. Where the hell was Alfbender? He slipped the pistol behind his thigh and let Raphael go ahead of him to the first platform.

Built on pilings driven into the clay and sand, the platform was made of split pine logs taken from the surrounding woods. A ramp led up to it, and a rotting handrail ran along three sides. The third side opened onto the rope and plank bridge. A post lamp gave light.

Raphael leapt up the ramp and did a handstand in the middle of the platform. He fell to his feet silently and smiled.

Blake came up fast. Over Raphael's head he could see two heavy ropes which were anchored to separate pilings. These heavy lines swung down into the dark where smaller ropes tied into them and connected the floorboard of the swinging bridge. The post light revealed only the first few feet of the bridge. The rest of it swung below the platform toward the blackness of the marsh and then up to the next wooden stand. Three dark stretches of bridge lay between the platforms and the bright Victorian pavilion.

Raphael butted his head into a lamp post. "You know what Plato said? He said there were four most valuable things: health, beauty, strength, and riches. I learned that out of one of your books. You had it underlined."

"Where'd you get the book?" Blake asked, thinking now that he had better hold Raphael here.

"Your daddy. He brung me those books. Come to see me in the State Hospital. Nice-looking man. Like all of us, real pretty. We talked and talked."

"You like Plato?" Blake got a good grip on the pistol. He'd tell him to lie down and aim to hit him in the leg if he didn't.

Raphael bent over as if to sit down, then soundlessly

somersaulted backward out the open side of the platform into the darkness of the bridge below.

Blake jumped toward the opening. He kept himself from yelling. He tried to speak calmly. "Come on, Raphael. Don't run off now. You said you wanted me to take you back to the hospital. If you don't wait for me, then the cops will have to do it."

"Strength's the most valuable gift. That's what I say to ole Plato. Being strong is good."

"Sure. I think . . . I think you're right there. Why don't you come on up in the light now."

Playing was just the best thing. There was no hurry now. He would get him to tag along. Just put sugar and honey in your voice.

"You said we could go to the pavilion."

"We can," Blake said. "I need to see you though. I don't like walking down into the dark."

"I'll be here. I'll be waiting."

Raphael was swinging on the bridge. Blake could hear the ropes straining against the platform. In his guts he got the shakes.

When Blake stepped off the platform onto the thin planks of the bridge, the light fell solidly behind him and the narrow length of the bridge swayed and sank. He caught his breath.

The wind rushed up from the marsh. Blake blinked his eyes against the wind tears. He stuck the pistol into his belt. Moving down now, he gripped the guide ropes on either side of him and felt salt on them. He was swinging out more now, and his belly fluttered. He tried to keep his hands tightly on the ropes and tapped ahead with the toes of his shoes. The angle of the bridge was dropping sharply, maybe sixty degrees now. His back strained to keep himself upright, and still the descent increased. With his feet he could feel the boards becoming slippery and fast. He was maybe twenty-five feet up from the marsh and tidal channel. But if he fell and hit in the muck he could survive—if Raphael was leading him down here to push him off. Where was Raphael's knife? The ropes stung his hands. Holding too tight. He loosened his grip. His eyes were tracking better and he felt now almost at the lowest part of the bridge. Hands to ropes. Feet carefully ahead. Easy. Easy.

Swinging out two feet to each side, he was down in the trough of the bridge. Here he waited. Below, the tide was cascading through the marsh grass. The ropes popped and whined. The post light felt very far behind him. He waited for Raphael. He moved a hand to his gun. Above him he could see the stars. The wind passed over his head and he did not feel cold. He was making it, by God! Standing here. Waiting on Raphael and whatever he had in the dark for him. Behind and before him there was light, but here he hung out alone over the marsh and he *was* ready to go on toward the second landing.

"Raphael! Raphael! Here I am. I'm down in the belly of it. Damn you! I'm at the lowest part, you bastard!" He forced a laugh and grabbed the ropes tightly and pounded his feet into the slats. He shook the whole bridge and laughed again. "Here! Here! Come and get me!"

Quiet. Stillness. Just the sound of the tide and the creaking bridge. Blake counted five red winks from a buoy. Settle down now. Okay. Keep the smartness in your hands and feet.

Up ahead two oak trees crowded the climbing half of the bridge. Moss trailed off them like rags. Fifteen feet beyond lay the second platform and light. The purity of light seen from below. He would get there. He just had to hold to the ropes and let his feet again judge ahead of him. But the trees worried him now. Raphael very surely could hide himself within the moss. Blake edged easily ahead and felt for his pistol and watched the trees so carefully. They did not appear as close to the bridge as he'd first thought. He could see the slats at least, the way the bridge moved on past the moss. The light from the second landing traced some silver in the trees, and he could make out the black trunks.

Turning his hands at angles, he began pulling himself up toward the oaks. Suddenly from below he heard the sound of something heavy splashing down into the water. He grabbed the ropes thinking Raphael had cut part of the bridge. Listening, he looked over the side and saw shafts of cattails and the back of a sandbar. Nothing else. The long snout of an alligator hurtled through his mind. But they kept a dreadful silence at night. Whatever troubled the dark was below. Go ahead, he told himself. Go on.

Now his gut sensed the trees and twisted. From here Blake inhaled their brief autumn odor: the dying of the leaves and dampness of the moss. He crept toward the first one, keeping his hands on the ropes behind him so he could spring back. Two feet away now. He searched the top, then the lower part of the trees, keeping his knees bent, ready. He reached out and touched the nearest cluster of moss: cold, damp. Feeling the tendrils acutely. Like small cutworms. Like live things hanging before him. Still no motion in the moss. No Raphael. The bridge here swayed much less now. He studied the distance to the wedge of light cast by the post lamp. He stretched his hands before him and squatted down to gather power in his legs. He rolled his head to each side, testing his balance. He breathed and sprang.

In the air he was off and felt it. When he landed, a rope slashed his face. His hands clawed for anything. The pistol clattered out of his belt and slid ahead of him. He threw his arms around the bridge and kicked his legs back up onto the slats.

His face was burning. He lay in the lamplight. The bridge felt stable. He laid his face against the damp wood and rested.

The pistol was caught at the edge of the ropes where they fastened into the slats. There would be no trouble in getting it. Just ease up now. He did not even need the gun so much. The pistol was not so necessary. What was a pistol? These lies made him move more smoothly. On hands and knees he approached. He had beaten the first tree. His face was hurting some, but he was glad of the pain because he was moving strongly in it. The slats arched into his knees and the palms of his hands. Two feet from the pistol. All at once the bridge bucked violently. One hand caught the ropes, the other reached out. The pistol slid off. He heard it clatter below. Then from somewhere very close he heard a squeaky laugh. His knees shot under him. He doubled his fists. Silence. From out toward the marsh he heard something running. A crashing. The laugh rose again, close and somewhere beneath him. It ticked on. A high mechanical laughter. A tapping in the throat.

"Ploosh said the gun to the water."

Raphael's voice. Nearby. Blake couldn't fix him. "I don't need the gun."

"But you carried it, and I think somewhere you did intend to use it."

"I had it with me is all."

"You sighted down on me good in them woods. You drew a bad bead on Raphael."

"Stand in some light!" Blake shouted.

"You're feeling them guts now, aren't you? They're in you. The family's intestines are bright. You keep on following me now. You keep showing me those nice guts."

Blake felt a sudden release. "I made it across, Raphael! And I'll make it to you!" He heard the laugh again. Then silence.

Let Raphael wait. Let him plan. Blake began moving again. He felt strong and good. Despite the long night and the weakness of his body, he was breaking his mother free.

Up on the second landing now. He felt the light shining on him. He looked in front and below him toward the darkness of the second bridge and then beyond to the last platform and bridge and finally the pavilion. Farther out lay the gray and black marsh and in the distance the first small lights of Port Sound. The canning factory's whistle blew four o'clock.

Again he stepped down into the rhythm of the bridge. He could feel his own weight pulling down the ropes. He gripped the guide ropes well again. He started gliding down the steep swaying of the bridge. No more caution. No hesitating. Silently. Strongly. Feeling the bridge and his muscles and the night give over to him. He *was* strong.

Going down the angle, ten feet farther into the dark, he first felt it. Overhead. A motion. He stopped in the gentle bobbing of the bridge. He saw only darkness and the next landing. But he sensed something twining just before his face. A turning in the dark like a current. He swept the air in front of him. Then he heard it: a clipping together like the thin sucking of membrane.

Blake pulled his hands back and squatted down. He tried to spot what was before him in silhouette against the last platform light. On his knees he saw nothing ahead or over him but darkness. But he still heard something, and now, with a change in the breeze, he sensed an odor and the same movement: twisting. He stood up and extended a hand, feeling: the cool air, the sense of salt in the air, and the thinnest debris of the night marsh. The motion seemed to stop. Suddenly he saw a flicker of light. A cinderlike burning. He fell back and wiped at his eyes. There was nothing there. There had to be nothing. He balanced in the small swells of the bridge, then darted forward.

Straight between his eyes the jaws struck him fast and sharp. Instinctively he blocked his face. Heard himself scream. Slickness, cold muscles, and the weight of the thing down on him, encircling his head. The jaws stung his chin. He caught hold of the body and smashed a fist against it. Tried to pull the coils away. He fell to the side of the bridge, jamming his neck against the ropes. Gripping the body, he yanked. A tiny squeal and hiss. Fluid squirted over his face and hands. He rolled to one side and went over. Feeling his hands reach out, his wind go. Falling. He sensed every cell go hard. The twisting of his spine as he tried to face the ground. Falling. Nothing below him. Hands trying to catch hold of the dark. Rolling over now. Trying to get over before he hit.

Never had the wind burst out of his gut so completely. As if a piling had driven through him. His gut was a hole. Smooth blackness. No feeling. Emptiness and no nerves in him. Hands grinding into the sand, tearing at the reeds. Squeezing them like straws leading to light and air. Something cold went cracking off in his ears. Pounding. Lines and dots. SOS and nothing.

He came up to a coldness running down his head, a warmth behind his neck. He heard his lungs sucking air, swelling enough to cut his breath again at his throat. His brains were busted out. Cold blood rushing down his neck now. Waiting for the last pictures of all his life to rise, then his eyes began to focus. Blurs at first. Outlines. A few things. Raphael.

"A little bit now. Just a little. You'll go out on so much air," Raphael said. He pressed back on Blake's rib cage, scooped up some water onto his forehead.

Blake moved his legs and arms. He did not hurt. Now he tried to turn. Initial pains flashing in his spine and shoulder. Where was Raphael now? Where the hell was he?

"Alright now. You're fine. Sip the air. Just let the good blood roll on through now."

Raphael appeared on his left. Blake tried to focus on him. Tried to watch him. Carefully Blake felt his neck. It was slick, grimy. He smelled a black sourness. He eased up on his elbows. Breathing was better. Vision. Raphael sat in front of him.

"Snake," Blake said. No lights jumped in the air. His hands jerked up toward his chin. "Jesus. I got bit."

Raphael smoothed a hand over Blake's hair. "No snake."

Blake raised up. Pains coupled. "You look for it. I broke it in half. It's all over me . . . you look."

Reaching behind him, Raphael picked up the long body. "Eel," he said.

Using his middle finger Blake traced the drooling mouth. The yellow eye. He slumped back to the ground. He placed his hands over his eyes.

He laid in the slowing rhythm of his heart, checking out his bones. Making everything move. He was hurting at last. Most of the pain seemed on the surface. When he looked up, Raphael's blue eyes were narrow and laughing.

Taking two swallows of air, Blake got on his elbows again. Raphael made no noise. His hair was shining in the light of the platform overhead.

"I was hanging under the first bridge and I fell in. Then I got the idea. I had some nice line in my pocket," Raphael said.

Raphael's hands. Empty.

"I hung him up there. I got down in the inlet and scooped him and tied him up there with my line. We did it when we were kids. When the moon got full and we had lots of beer in us."

Blake laid back down in the marsh. He was weak. He was hurting and too damn weak.

I'm going to get you up in that pavilion now. Up in the light I'll lay you down on them planks and cut open your steamy guts. No, your brain. That's right. The frontal lobe.

Blake felt Raphael's hands take him by the shoulders, lift him up. "Let go. I got something busted. Let go."

Raphael pointed to a ladder on the side of the pavilion. "I'll carry you up there. We can check it out."

Blake's head was spinning. He had to get a couple of feet

away from Raphael. He had to watch his hands. In the light he'd be safer. In the pavilion.

Blake stumbled up to the ladder. He was scared now. Adrenaline cleared up his head a little, gave him some strength. Raphael's hands pushed him. He climbed up.

Top of the ladder. Light. Raphael shoved him over. He fell onto a bench, pulled his legs down. Everything was still hazed, but Blake could see the floor, green lattice, and benches. He sat up and worked his jaws and breathed. He felt Raphael slip down beside him.

Raphael laid his head back on the bench and pointed out toward the sky. "What do you think's up there?" he asked softly.

At first Blake thought not to answer. Save your energy. No—talk a little. "No wind, now."

"Maybe something else though. Maybe spirits."

"Night's over. We're alright."

"Things moving around. Powers and dominions."

"Who can tell," Blake said.

If he could keep his left hand close to Blake that might bring him a little comfort, feeling of warmth: safety. He could stab him with his right. Not his natural movement. Slower on impact. But the right would deliver him the wound. "Your mother has some prime notions about what's beyond the dark, you know? She's got some pretty arrangements in her head."

Blake felt Raphael's hand casually bump against his thigh.

"A graveyard of angels. You ever hear her speak of it?"

Blake saw the pistol sticking out of Raphael's belt.

The filed razor felt so sharp. Very long and very much a red puncture sort of feeling. He would hit the throat and have some fun there. After he talked some. Talking to good natures always felt so honorable. "See, elephants sense when they are about to die and move toward some valley where all their kind put themselves down. Jess said angels had a similar place."

Blake looked at Raphael's eyes. Now he saw what had always been there. The unholy cold. The thinking dark.

"She said there came a time for them when they realized nothing worked for them anymore. When they knew to lay down their tusks. Huge angels."

Blake felt Raphael's hand move closely beside his own. Warm. Just touching. He glanced down and saw a razor in Raphael's left hand, then he looked out at the dark.

"Your mother built the place so beautifully in her head. Vines and valleys and the rivers in between like wine. And each angel has his own alabaster slab. His own bed lying in the valleys and the green. Jess said the angels would become all full of death and then go seek out their place, wings dragging behind them. Their faces beautiful but sad and all of them still singing. Hymns coming out of them weakly. They would find their place and just lie down. Folding their wings. And they looked up toward the darkness and breathed out a starry breath and went away. Though their bodies stayed perfect. Such beautiful creatures. Tricksters and warriors. Some philosophers and musicians. Thousands of them lying there. Glowing, silent, and all their parts losing light except their blue eyes and faces holding up the sky . . ."

Blake had fixed his eyes on the pistol. He felt Raphael slide very close to him.

"You know what? I laid with your old man, too. Me and your daddy," Raphael whispered, knife in motion.

Blake yanked the pistol away.

A blink went across Raphael's eyes and his lips opened. Blake pulled the trigger and the blast threw Raphael backwards. The blood ran down his forehead onto his cheeks and neck. Blake held the gun exactly. Raphael's eyes did not move. There was blood and splintered bone behind him on the bench. Blake reached toward him and Raphael slipped from the bench to the floor. He lay face up. The clear eyes were filling with blood.

Blake knelt beside Raphael. He felt his throat and then his chest. He pushed down his lower lip and saw the white teeth there. When he removed his finger, the lip slowly drew back up.

With his left hand Blake pulled down Raphael's jaw. He stuck his index finger under the tongue. Soft tissue. Red gums. Saliva turning cold. Where was his own feeling? He waited for something to flood through him. Nothing came.

Blake bent over Raphael. With his thumb he wiped blood out of the soft eyes. He scrutinized the face. A small scar at the corner of his mouth. Blond beard just budding out. New lines near the eyes. Five freckles across the width of the nose. He brushed back the straw hair. It still felt alive. Gently he inserted a finger into one of Raphael's ears. He sat and looked at the bloody eyes. He kept his finger in the warm ear wax.

Out in the marsh there was the most delicate indication of dawn. No light yet, but movement. The sound of awakenings.

Blake saw the blood on his hands. His trousers. The floor was streaked in it. A pool was turning dark by the corpse's head. He grabbed the arms and dragged the body toward the ladder. He managed the bench, then bent the legs and swung them over the ladder. He listened. Everything still quiet. He moved in behind the corpse, straddled it with his legs, and pushed his groin against the head and shoulders. When it started sliding down he caught one arm and then followed. The head bumped along the rungs. The feet caught now and again and kept him from being pulled down by the weight.

On the ground Blake listened again. Crickets and the last tree frogs. Wind and a truck grinding far away. He had to go farther into the marsh. Where people didn't hunt. Where they couldn't see this thing. He bent down and dragged the body behind him. Going north now. Going toward the tidal creeks where the blue crab fed in silence.

Twenty feet away from the pavilion the real marsh began. When he was a boy he had been afraid of this place. He needed it now. He switched grips. Got another handful of hair. The thing wasn't so heavy. Water began seeping through his shoes. Lots of scrub oak ahead. Marsh grass was a lighter color than the oaks and tall as his head. He could feel sand giving way to mud under his feet and the marsh grass closing in on him. Blackberry briers were tearing into his clothes. He stopped and looked behind. He could see the pavilion light through thin bars of marsh grass and clusters of oak, but the platform lights were blocked out now.

He breathed in the fecund marsh. Red roots and runnels of thin silt and the rich gumbo of mildews and molds and the black stinking cavities of palmettos. But beyond lay a tidal creek. He went on and gratefully felt the warm water cover the tops of his shoes. Up ahead he could make out the black wall of cypresses. Shells crunched under his feet and the mud hissed each time he raised a foot. His back and forearm began a dull stiffness and ache. The sweat was cutting into his eyes. He wiped it away. Sweat was good. No fever when you sweat. His legs were hurting, but the mud was deeper and getting cool. Tidal mud.

Suddenly something rammed painfully into his thigh. Blake cried out. He let go of the corpse. A cypress knee had sheared off in him. Bending to his left, he slipped a palm down into the mud and pulled his left knee under him and sat down. He straightened his right leg. He felt for the splinter. It was not long and was just under the skin. He pinched the butt of the splinter and jerked. The wood slipped out easily. No pain. He split his trouser leg open and probed the wound. No more wood. He pressed his hand against the wound then drew up his right leg and rested his head on his knee. Now everything in him was hurting. All of his muscles stove up in pain and he became aware of thirst: dry, needle-point thirst way down in his throat all the way to his guts, and too he had to piss. His sides hurt from it. He tried to get up, couldn't make it. He felt the first of the urine split out of him, just a weak painful thread, and then the remainder poured out and it felt fine going down his legs and over his butt.

He looked up at the sky. Still black, but no stars now. He turned. Mud covered the corpse and he couldn't really see the face anymore. He grabbed the body by the collar and then hoisted himself up by a sapling. It took both hands to drag the body now. The marsh felt like it was rocking under his feet. When he started moving again his head reeled. He kept going toward the cypresses. His vision had gotten worse, as if he were seeing through a screen, as if the air were thatched black-white. Without seeing them, he stumbled into a bank of cattails. A white heron cried and rose into the air. He was close now. Herons fished the channels where the big blues fed. He crashed through the dry cattails. They rattled and blew feathers into his face, light down across his cheeks.

Coming out of the cattails, he tripped and fell. His cheek laid against something dry. He reached his hands out before him. Sand. Smooth and packed hard. He smiled. He rubbed his face into the sand. It smelled straight and lean as wood. Rising up on his knees, he could make out the first saltwater creek just beyond the sandbar. He reached behind him and for the last time caught hold. Dragging the body behind him he crawled toward the canal. He dug his right elbow into the sand and kicked with his bad leg. The first tendrils of sea grass. The black holes of sea worms. Now fiddler crabs. Hundreds. He left the corpse and crawled to the edge of the creek, then stretched his palms out over the water to cup its surface. The silent dark of the water. He wet his face. Soon the tide would be going out, funneling through the sand. Could Raphael ride out with the tide? He'd never be found. What if he was? Who was Raphael?

Blake turned to see the fiddlers had covered the corpse. He got up and dragged the body toward the creek. The ocean. All things connect. Let it be the sea's decision: the South China Sea or the southern blue crab. Teetat crabbed these shallows. Teetat! At the edge of the water as he held the body against his chest, he thought dimly of Teetat's fish camp that must be nearby. He felt the water's chill only when he released the corpse and imagined its slow sinking: to the current he didn't know.

Minutes passed before he found himself once more on the bank of the creek. The light might have warmed him, or at least brought him to, for in the distance he immediately recognized the orange lamp of Teetat's shack several hundred yards away. He was able to skirt the winding creek but not the marsh, and when he banged on the screen door his knuckles had no feeling. A second door opened. Painful light. The scarred face.

He collapsed.

When Blake awoke he didn't know the room. He threw down his hands, then felt a dry palm go into his own.

Teetat patted Blake's side and easily broke his grip. He handed Blake a quart jar of water.

The water rumbled down into Blake's belly. He could not move. He lay in the bed and looked at Teetat's bony face, the always distant, inscrutable eyes. For an instant he looked like a Chinaman. The room was fluttering with kerosene lamp light. Newspapers were tacked on the walls. The room was full of rusting crab traps.

Teetat pulled a pear from a bucket. He laid it on his knee. He took a fish knife from his pocket and split the fruit open. "Want some food?"

Blake closed his eyes.

"Want something to eat?"

Blake looked down at his clothes. Different pants, shirt.

Teetat dropped the pear back into the bucket. He rose and

went to a small table. He had his back to Blake. A match
went off.

Blake could smell the marijuana.

Teetat came back to the chair beside the bed. He sat and
took a few tokes. He did not look at Blake. He held the joint
about eye level, brought it in to puff, then held it out again.

Blake felt his eyes sting. They stopped. He blinked away
the trace of water in his eyes.

Teetat looked up at him then. He whistled in the dope.
Bending down, he drew a bottle from beneath the bed, un-
screwed the cap, and put it to Blake's lips.

Blake swallowed once.

Teetat pulled the bottle away and waited, then set it to
Blake's lips again.

The vodka burned all the way down.

Teetat returned the bottle beneath the bed. He finished his
joint and then held Blake's right hand and looked beyond him
into the newsprint of the wall.

Blake shut his eyes again and saw nothing. For a while he
was near nothing, then his body jerked, woke him. Teetat let
go of his hand. Blake got up on the side of the bed. The rope
cut in his face hurt more than anything else. He was dizzy.
He found his shoes, got them on.

Teetat pointed beside the bed. The pistol lay on the floor.
Blake reached down and picked it up. He held it, then slid it
back into his pocket. He rose from the bed, steadied himself.
"What time is it?"

"After five."

"How do I get out of here?"

"I always take the outgoing tide."

Blake easily found the path that meandered along the creek
to station six, the last stop before Cane Island. When Blake
arrived, the trolley car was on its return toward Port Sound.
He got on. He rode through the city and then back, his mind
a haze until he neared the island again.

The trolley car rattled along busily. Blake's temperature felt very low now, probably around ninety-six. He felt cold and his heart went on very dully. Just before his stop he went to the front of the car to the conductor. He had slicked hair and a shiny nose. He was dragging off a Lucky and reading the *Morning News*.

"Could I bum a couple of those?" Blake asked.

The conductor sent his eyes down the line and then at Blake. He handed over a pack. Blake took two. The conductor was mumbling and still reading, so Blake took the matches inside the cellophane as well. He set the pack on the change box.

"You read this?" The conductor wiped a finger across his nose. He held the paper up.

Blake just shook his head.

"He was a good trainman. He kept everything working and clean. Somebody laid one through his head and kicked him in the river. Some bastard done him no good. He had all his dimes on him, too."

"Sorry," Blake said.

"Knew him ten years. Maybe more." The conductor noticed Blake sliding the cigarettes into his pocket. "You're not smoking those?"

The conductor had a little accusation in his eyes.

"Just waiting to smoke outside," Blake said. "Do you miss your friend?"

"I'm more sensitive than most about these things. I'll probably be feeling low about it for a few days. I'll take a bad headache and all."

"It's okay," Blake said. He put a hand on the man's shoulder.

Withdrawing into his booth, the conductor coughed and jiggled the tiller. "I'm looking forward though. An optimist is me. Yep, I'm looking on to the future when the guy that got ole Doug gets his. When that fella gets burned, I'll feel better," the conductor said. He slowed the trolley down for the island stop.

Blake stepped down to the door. "Feel better," he said.

"You too," said the conductor. "Where the hell you been, boy? You look like you've had a night of it."

"I borrowed your matches here," Blake said.

"Alright. I'm glad you told me. I'll always pardon an honest man."

Blake got off the trolley and walked down the street. When he got inside the gate of the driveway he sat down by a pecan tree. He lit a Lucky Strike and puffed. He did not inhale. He took a couple more puffs and laid his head back against the tree and wept. He bared his teeth and strained hard and felt everything running out his face.

A car passing down the causeway hit him with its lights. He straightened up. He wiped his face and smoked the last cigarette. On the pecan tree he rubbed the last butt dead.

Moving up to the house, he saw all the lights still burning. He came around to the side porch where the fig bushes hugged the house. Jess was sitting out on the steps. Electric light was behind her.

"Who the hell is that?" she yelled, whiskey much in her voice.

"Nobody special."

"The hell you are. Get in front of my eyes, mister."

Blake stepped forward.

"Well, what the hell do you want?"

"I'm just coming home."

"Yeah, well that's down the road and over the creek, buster, 'cause you don't belong here."

"What are you doing out here so late, Jess? You should have slept some."

"I know," she answered. "I came out to brush my hair and take a little of the hooch. Want a sip?"

"No."

"Why not? You're a damn drunk or something worse."

Blake moved steadily toward her.

"I think I smell a Birddog now," Jess said uneasily.

"It's me. It's Buckles."

"It's not. It's cunning. Now, could it be that Raphael has come back from the dark?"

Blake said nothing.

"Well, let me tell you something, pal, you better—"

"Mama," Blake said quietly.

Jess put the bottle down beside her. "Come on up in the light then."

Blake held his hands out.

Jess gave a short cough, pinched an index finger on either side of her nose, and slid them down to her chin. Her hair hung down below her shoulders and her face seemed without makeup and outdone. "Where do sons go so late at night?"

Just sitting down beside her Blake felt relief and acceptance. The beginning of pardon. "You said some harsh things and I went to walk them off."

Jess sighed and looped an arm around his shoulders. "What we have here in her gin and fallen hair—what we have is Mother. Someone not to be lied to."

Not even the least linkage in him gave way. He commanded respect of all his parts. "I had a walk."

"In the marsh?" She pointed at his shoes.

"Yep, I went into the marsh."

"Hunting Raphael?"

"He'd been fooling around the house."

"Alfbender told me. Did you find him?"

"Yes."

"Was he the monster you thought?"

"I think he was, Mama."

"Well?"

"I sent him away."

"Alfbender had the cops out here. We looked around. The cops are still looking."

"Don't you worry now. Don't you fret about it." Blake

brushed back a strand of her hair. She was very drunk. As always the words came out well, but she was in a fog.

Jess turned his chin to the light. "You're cut. You're hurt, honey. Did he try something on you?"

"He tried. But we talked about things and I let him go. He was more sane than he seemed." A sudden feeling came to Blake: He hated Raphael.

Jess rocked him against her breast. "So what seems—is not. The old lesson."

Blake pulled away from her embrace. "I want you to get a suitcase now. Try to take just one. We can move a lot quicker."

Jess patted her thighs. "My luggage *does* travel so poorly these days."

She dug some pins from her blouse pocket and stuck them into her mouth. She began rolling up her hair.

"Did you ever hear from the agent?" Blake asked.

"I did. Why, I got the part, Buckles. The agent sent the telegram here and I'm just so excited about it all."

Blake squeezed her waist. "You got your dream. You have it. Now you can be finished with all of this."

"Of course, there's no hurry. Rehearsals don't begin for another week."

"No waiting. We're going straight to the train. I'll send you up all you need. We have about an hour," Blake said.

"A week is not a burden. It's not so hard on me."

"It's time enough for the family to get you." Blake took a couple of pins from her lips and helped to fix her hair. It felt warm and abiding in his hands. Your mother's hair is life. "You broke them tonight, right? You let them know."

"Cross summoned some fine psychology against me."

"Which you beat."

"Millis willy-nillied and cajoled."

Blake tucked her hair as neatly as he could into a bun and pinned it. He kissed her hair and her victory and her new life. "I want you to know I'm proud of you, Mama. The way you waded into this night. The way you took on everything and won."

"I just have so much booze in me."

"Coffee will wash it out."

"I have to say good-bye. I must go in and sit a while."

"Coffee, a kiss, and bye," Blake said.

"You sound very different somewhere. You sound hard."

"I'm tired. I have some fever cooking," Blake said.

Jess rose from the steps. "I want to be happy, Buckles. See it on my face? I want to be everything you want me to. How do I look?"

"East Side." Blake smiled.

"Are my eyes right? Is my smile strong?"

"You're fine now."

"Good. I'm on my way now. One suitcase is all I need. Just a suitcase and some coffee. I'm so happy."

"You go in ahead of me. Pack up. I want to sit out here a minute. I'll drink some coffee with you in a while."

Jess kissed his chin and went in the house.

He sat down in the shadows of the house, out of the light. His eyes were aching a lot and his legs had those pains which meant his fever would burn high today. He laid his head down on his arms. Raphael's face rose from the water. He pushed the thought under.

When he opened his eyes he found Alfbender sitting beside him polishing his piccolo. "How'd you learn to be so damn quiet?"

"Chickasaw blood," said the lawyer.

"Jess blow them out while I was gone?"

"They had a ball. They truly had a good time."

Blake shook Alfbender by his clavicle. "She's packing, Alf. They've been beat for sure this time."

"Are you alright, Blake?"

"I'm strong."

170

"So what happened to you and Raphael?"

"Tough things."

"I lost you in the woods."

"O mighty Chickasaw tracker," Blake said.

"What happened?"

"I shot him through the head."

"Jesus!"

"I left him in one of those creeks by Teetat's."

"Did anybody see you?"

"Somebody could have heard the shot maybe."

"We'll have to go get him. He'll get found there."

Blake was quiet.

Alfbender tugged Blake's calf. "There ain't enough crabs to pick him clean. And maybe the tide's not strong enough to pull him on out either. I'll think of something."

"Will you?"

"I'll figure a way."

Blake shivered a little, then drew his muscles taut. "How do you feel about me?"

"I'm here. I'm with you."

"Jess doesn't know about Raphael. Let's let her leave with some hope."

"I *hope* she goes to the rails, Blake. I hope she does that."

"We'll be on that seven o'clock train."

"I don't know anything about the trains here. I'm superstitious. I stay away from them."

"Things are working out," Blake said.

Alfbender raised his eyebrows and stowed his piccolo in his pocket. "I'll be waiting here for you."

If there had been a warmer, more secure time for Blake in this house it had passed deeply away with dreams and fairy tales. Standing in the hall, the wood and the glass of the doors, the brass handles and bumps and scars of years, the bountiful migrations of familiar hearts and bones and exquisite blood and all their finery beckoned him to be at peace, here, now. To find one of the deep beds and dreaming quilts and ease himself into sleep, into staying and becoming part of what was natural for him: the knowledge of his own kin.

He could hear laughing down the hall, in the family room. He wondered if they had found any of Raphael's cipherings, if they had sensed in some way what was so very near to them. Pausing just outside the door, he felt as if he were about to betray them. He rapped the pane.

Cross had the sincere light of the family room strictly behind him. "Blake, we're about to swap a few stories. Looks like you could use a stout drink. Come on in. We need you."

Blake thought of taking off his muddy shoes. There was no time now.

Millis and Jess were sitting defensively close together on the couch. Hunting dogs and quail posed in pictures behind them. Millis wore a fluffy robe and her spectacles hung from her neck.

"I apologize for"—Blake made a motion at his shoes—"for this."

Millis hopped up and fixed a saucer of doughnuts and cake. Her earlobes jiggled. Her fighting eyes seemed to bid him only good. "Not mincing words as usual, I'll tell you that you look like death on a back burner and smell worse. Never mind though. Just eat up. Your mother told us you went out for a walk and that's fine and what a boy should do on Halloween." She handed him the plate and patted his neck.

Cross meanwhile had pulled up a cane-bottom chair. He sat Blake down, handing him a mug of coffee. He wore his vest and white shirt. His neck was rich and florid, his hair perfectly pressed, his eyes full of unspeakable mercy. "Fit for a prince now. The young lord come home to roost." He lit a cigarette and, carrying his glorious cloisonné cup, arranged himself next to Jess.

She now did not seem so well to Blake. He saw that he had

done a lousy job on her hair, and though she smiled at him, showing her dark teeth and the tendons of her neck, all beneath her eyes seemed worn and on its knees, and her eyes themselves lay full of alcohol and capillaries and a little girl's despair.

Propping his shoes up on a table, Cross waved a perfumed hand. "I remember when we were children and Mother would let us stay up all night on Halloween, just like this. She'd stand us in front of that mirror right there and help us out of our costumes."

"Reciting, remember?" Millis said. "We came out of the costumes making our speeches."

Cross slapped a hand on his chair. "That's right. The eve of all souls. Remember the saints, she said. Every year we had to memorize a new life. I liked Peter. The fisherman. Did your mother ever tell you who she liked best, Blake? Did she ever tell you who she played almost every year?" Cross asked.

"I never heard about this," Blake said. He felt them building again. The construction of something very coarsely in their faces.

"Tell him, sister," Cross said, putting an arm around Jess.

"It was just a ritual we had. It was part and parcel of Mother," Jess said.

"Cross always objected," Millis said, holding her rosy bare feet in her hand.

Cross was rubbing Jess's neck, his breath short and full of gin. "Huitzilopochtli is who I always wanted to be. The Blue Hummingbird. I've always been a pagan at heart." He laughed and laid his face along Jess's.

She looked pale and very much trapped to Blake. Her hands had wrenched themselves into freckled balls. The veins rose stiffly in them.

"Don't look so cynical, Blake," Cross said. "It was a family time. A time to gather round and be close and loving of one another. Just like tonight."

"You spend too much time remembering," Blake said, very aware of the soundness of his voice and aware too of how they took it.

"A family *is* a memory," Cross said plainly.

"More than a memory, I think. The present. The future. But much more than memory," Blake said.

"It was a celebration of life. A party," Millis said. "Mother made it up for Jess, really. She was the baby. She was the unexpected beauty in our lives. In Mother's."

"It wasn't so bad, honey," Jess said. "It was a nice time. We took off our costumes and told the saints' lives to one another. We had some cocoa and cookies late at night and shed off a lot of bad things. I was Saint Teresa. I was the little flower."

"Do you remember any of your speech?" Millis asked Cross.

"Indeed I do," Cross said and went to stand before the full-length mirror. "I am Saint Peter. I was a fisherman. I knew the waters and the depths. I could throw a net and snare the catch. Let's see . . . something, something . . . and I denied the one who loved me best three times. But still he took me back and I was loved more than before."

Millis applauded lightly.

"I can even remember some of what I said." Jess spoke softly. Her face and eyes seemed at low levels.

Cross moved out of her way and she sat before the mirror. Her mouth sent up a smile. "I am Saint Teresa. I am the little flower. In all the days I grew and grew. I was filled by love. In the nights I sleep with my sisters. In the days I work by them. We are the light in the breeze and the glory of the stones. Together we are the beauty and the grace. Together we are all blossoms and melodies and we will never die."

"Lovely," Cross said. He poured some more gin into her glass. He lit a cigar and set it between her lips.

Jess toked the cigar once. "I don't feel so happy anymore. I don't feel very well at all."

174

"Sugar, don't worry, now. It's just late," Cross said. "Let brother put you to bed. It's time for us all to sleep."

Blake found himself up very quickly. "Jess, do you have your bag?"

His uncle's eyes hit him fast.

Jess blocked her elbows into her sides.

"How many ounces did you pour?" Blake asked.

"I think your fever has worn you down, Buckles," Millis said. "You better go on to your room now."

Blake was heading toward Jess when Cross stopped him. "Just let her sleep and recover. The night's been rough here. Too much hurrahing."

Blake met his uncle's eyes and said nothing.

"Are you high on something, son?" Cross asked.

"What are you going to do, lock *me* up? Send me to the asylum?"

"You're afraid you're sick, aren't you, son? It's haunting you, I know. Both your parents unstable. Your mother an alcoholic. These things drum you down and sometimes you become what you fear, but—"

"I'm not who you think."

Cross caught him by the arm. He spoke very carefully. "If you try to take her out of a sickbed . . . if you try to hurt her because of something rotten in yourself, I'll take you down there."

Millis slipped out of the room.

"Now your Aunt Millis has gone to call the doctor just to settle you down and make you see that your mother needs us and she needs you."

Jess sat on the floor and remained silent.

"Are you willing to knock me down?" Blake said.

Cross edged his feet to a different angle. "You just stay very still, young man. You just wait."

"No waiting," Blake said and jammed the pistol into Cross's side. "I *can*," he whispered.

Cross lost power in his eyes.

With his left, Blake pushed his uncle to the side. "Come on, Mama." He reached his hand down into hers and pulled her up.

Jess rose and her eyes moved into Blake.

"I intend good things," Blake said.

Cross set his hands in his pockets and squared his shoulders. "You'll spend some time in the Williams Building. I won't have you go to jail because I love you, Blake . . ."

"And because I'm beautiful and needed and I am a member of this family." Blake walked over to him. "And if you ever tell me that again I think I'll blow your eyes out."

"Blake, you get yourself quiet inside and remember who you are now," Jess said.

"You'd really like to throw me in the nut house, wouldn't you, Uncle Cross?"

"I do what the moment merits."

Blake shoved him backward.

Cross picked up his coffee cup and sipped, smiling. "Your father was deranged. The hospital records are full of it. I'll slip some cake to you through the bars on your birthday."

Blake smashed the cup from his hands.

Coffee and shattered enamel splattered Cross. He caught a few pieces in his hand. "I'll fry your brains out down there. In six months I'll have you licking envelopes for the company."

The pistol fitted neatly under his uncle's jaw.

At last Blake saw the snake in his uncle's face. For years it had hidden so well beneath his eyes. To see evil clearly was to hate it. "See, Mother. There it is—pried out of its hole. The sorrow of our lives." He felt Jess's hand go over his. He heard her whispering.

"Come on now. No, no. Outside. We need to go outside. Millis has called somebody by now."

"Do you know I could do it?" Blake asked.

"I know," said Jess.

"Are you sure you understand?"

"I see. Mama sees. Come on," Jess mumbled.

With his index finger, Blake tapped his uncle's head. "SOS, old man. SOS. You came so damn close and you don't even know it." He backed away and felt Jess moving behind him.

"Watch your step going down the road," Cross said.

Blake could tell he was afraid. "We're gone and safe. Or so you better hope."

Moving down the hall, Blake snatched a coat off the hall tree and handed it to Jess. "You put this on. It's cooler now."

Alfbender met them just as they were going out. All three of them stepped onto the porch. There was light in the air. Blake could just make out the trees. The light looked as if it waited behind them.

"You headed out?" the lawyer asked.

"Pulled a gun on Cross," Blake said.

"You didn't hit him or anything?"

"I just let him know some things."

Alfbender swept his long hair back over his collar. "Can you make it to the tracks, Jess?"

"Sure I can," Jess said.

"The kid get tough with Cross?"

When she did not answer, Alfbender turned to Blake. "Now, if you did, he'll be burning. You go fast for that train. He'll have cops or somebody else looking for you. I got a feeling you turned over the wagon in Uncle Cross."

"Can I borrow your watch?"

Alfbender gave it to him.

"Look here," Alfbender said. His black eyes carried warmth and no fooling. "If anything screws loose in this thing now . . ." He paused and looked down at Jess's feet. "If anything blows cater-cornered, you just remember to stay down in yourself. Don't go climbing way high in yourself and expect everybody to be up there with you. Don't get all alone in yourself, now."

Blake nodded. "You going to the creek and take care of things?"

"Right there for a look and then I'll meet you at the yards. Now, you keep what I said straight, okay?"

Alfbender's heart was showing. Blake hugged him. When he stood back, the light was a thread stronger. "Things are alright now."

"Get on, then."

"I'll temper your brother, Jess," Alfbender called after her. "You make good time. You haven't seen everything tonight. You and your boy make honest time now."

"Sure," Jess said, and she did not look him in the face.

Blake felt the departing earth straight through his shoes and up to his head. He patted Jess on the hand. Fatigue was coming in on him now. Black spots floated over his eyes, but beyond the discomfort of his body, he felt high. He had kept his promise and Jess was free from the darkest of worlds. She was probably afraid and striking badly down in her belly because she had no clothes, nothing that a lady needed to carry with her. She would feel bad because she was being sent out very bare and hurriedly into her dream. So the idea came upon him naturally and sweetly. He stopped just before the trolley station.

"Mama, you're walking awful quiet over there," he said.

The light was coming in better. The dawn. Her face seemed cast down, her lips set at the corners. The air had sobered her some.

"I'm just thinking, honey."

"Worrying?"

"I'm going out with no money to some place I haven't seen in years. I don't have nothing with me."

"I'm going with you," Blake said. "We're getting on that train hand in hand. Riding off into the big dawn." Blake grinned.

She dropped the green of her eyes just beneath his own. "Well . . . I think that's fine."

Blake lifted up her chin. "There's to be no worrying now. Alfbender will send some money. I've got enough on me for the train. No more threats. No more asylums. And I have a notion in a couple years you'll be stealing light from Broadway."

Jess smiled and covered her mouth so the bad teeth would not show.

"I'm going to fix those teeth too."

"Oh, honey, don't you—"

"First stop in New York is the dental parlor, and I'll have you smiling like a Steinway." Blake circled his hands about her waist and swung her around. "We've beat them, Mama. Dear God, how we've outsmarted them all!"

They could hear the trolley car grinding toward them, just past station six.

"Well, your uncle loved his painted cup an awful lot. We better catch this trolley." At the station, they just made it.

Blake put his forehead against a windowpane. Dawn finished the marsh to a wasted gray and brown. The violent green of scrub oak, swamp gums of less color, and the failing white of the cattails. To the east the sun outlined the platforms and ropes of the hand bridges. The latticed pavilion sat empty and unmarked. Already the cypresses were beneath them. Blake looked back for the creek. He saw several black lanes of water. He could not tell which one. The car passed beyond the cypresses and now headed down into the city, and Blake felt nothing for the night.

The trolley made several stops in the city, then hurried up the trestle and crossed the harbor.

Blake and Jess stepped off on the north bank. The trolley car went no farther out during rush hour. It wheeled back toward downtown. Below them the harbor rumbled in work. Small fishing boats made even way toward the ocean. The wide-transomed ferry seemed elegant in the water. The light opened up the harbor and chiseled at the shadows of the docks. White cranes bobbed down for fish, and in the air gulls swept across the channel and rode the sea breeze out to sand-bars where the early minnows were breaking. Ship whistles climbed into the air. Buoys were ringing. Workers walked the gray docks, and the tide drew from the salt pools of the night and the angles of marsh grass. Then up channel, a vest of night still behind her, Blake saw silent motion. The lights burned on her bridge. She appeared to be a freighter, though she was stripped down to bare decks and rode high in her waters. No tugboat lined her. Her wake was clean.

"Do you see her?" Blake whispered.

Jess's eyes went wide. "Now, there's beauty. Now, there's grace," she said. "You know what your father told me once? Oh, I had not seen a ship all lit up in years. He told me it was not a ship at all but a friendly pilgrim. A great celestial pil-grim who, having finished with his nightly post, now slipped past our homes to sleep."

As the ship came closer, Jess turned sideways. "Ever since then I have never liked to see the faces on them. Somehow I'd rather believe that they are bright things who just sail out and never touch us again." She placed her hands over her eyes.

"I think I remember something you used to do for me at the end of bad times." Blake opened the locket of ambergris about her neck. He rubbed his thumbs into the cream, then circled them over his mother's eyelids. Her face began to gain color.

"Now, you just sit right beside me and close your eyes, too," she said.

Blake felt her index fingers searching for his eyes. He took her thumbs and placed them upon his eyelids. The ambergris felt cool. The movement of her thumbs seemed the very right and good motion now. He sat holding her fragile hands, feeling the presence of the ship as it silently swept by.

"It's good not to have to see the faces," Jess said.

"In a way," said Blake.

"How far down do you think she's gone?"

"Not too far."

"Can we wait a while? Can we not look yet?"

"You know that."

"You're going to let me keep a few dreams, aren't you?"

"Every one. Every good one. Don't you know that?"

"Sometimes you have to hold on to the bad ones as well. They keep you temperate."

"If they don't bind you. If they don't cause remorse."

"Some of us need remorse, Buckles."

"Not here, though. Not between me and you."

"Do you remember how to make the whippoorwill call?"

"That's a funny thing to ask."

"Can you still do it the way I showed you?"

Blake cupped his hands and blew into them. A low sound. He shifted the shape of his hands and the column of his air. The tone came out very clearly. He wavered the air in his throat and fluttered his hands slightly. Then he heard Jess begin to search for the right pitch. She found it more quickly and sounded high and clear. They sat side by side, eyes cool and shut, and cried like whippoorwills across the harbor.

"The whippoorwill has a very sad song. You'd say that, right?" Jess asked, breaking off first.

"I'd forgotten I could do this," Blake said.

"Well, there's some kind of remorse that is as lovely, as needed as that kind of song. Some of us are whippoorwills. We love the sadness of it all."

Blake wiped the traces of the ambergris from his eyes and found his mother searching him directly. He glanced down channel and saw only the stern of the ship. He jumped to the railing. "Good luck to you!" he shouted. "Good luck, way out there!"

"Do you see what I mean about sadness? About the beauty of it?"

"Remember the black spaces in your head. Remember the dead neurons, Mother."

Blake started toward the railway station. It lay five blocks down and to the right of the old railroad yards. Jess followed and said nothing to him, and he felt unpardonable.

Blake's eyes were burning steady now and he could feel the heat resting in his head and the weakness in his spine and the hard pains of his joints. The fever would pitch to a hundred and three today—near delirium, but he didn't mind going under the coals some place in North Carolina on a fast train. His watch read six-fifteen. They had half an hour. Easy time now.

"I don't think we should be on this open road," Jess said.

"I made an impression on Cross," said Blake.

"He could just come sweeping right up. There would be no problem."

"Not for me."

Jess turned suddenly. "You think you're really rough, don't you?"

"I'm not trying to be anything."

"You don't stick a pistol in your uncle's gut."

"The wind smells good. A sea wind. It's got the deep water currents in it," Blake said.

"It stinks. I think the damn wind stinks."

"Look, I know you're tired. I know things feel bad now. I'm not any better. I got sand all over me and fever and cockleburs in my socks." He hung an arm around her neck. "It'll be fine now. We'll have a drink and bunk up. Just take it easy on me, Mama."

Jess shrugged off his arm. When Blake saw her face he felt afraid. It was the face of battle. The metal eyes and grim mouth. The color of wrath.

"What if I said I didn't want to go? What would you say then?"

He had no answer. Ahead glared the broken stacks of the

yard. She did not understand. She was so tired probably. He had been careless and coarse with her.

"What the hell have you acquired tonight that allows you to push me so hard?"

"I saw some bad things. I kept a promise."

"How noble. How pure and true."

"What I am doing is good. It's a—quest."

"Don't use that kind of sleight of hand on me, kiddo. You're *afraid* to leave. It's the same old gutlessness in you. You're scared to go, so you're dragging good ole Mom to the big city so she can show you the ropes."

Still she had the power. Still she could take whole levels of confidence in him and twist them until he couldn't see and his mind broke down in static.

"Maybe you're retarded. That has occurred to me on occasion—that perhaps you're just a little slow. As a child you fumbled at your Lincoln Logs."

He increased his pace toward the front gate of the new spur. "I'm showing you my strong self now. It's new. It came real hard for me." Blake wanted to say this, but did not. He tried to keep desperation out of his face.

Jess was going at him sharply now. He blocked by looking up toward the railway buildings: shattered walls. The skylights burst and fallen. Racks and pulleys hanging blackly in the dawn. The enormous station and towers and broken causeways: stone holes of darkness and pointless stairs of bricks and last sills of fourth-floor rooms, high and balancing in the air, only wires and lath, even the plaster stripped away.

Behind him Blake heard car doors slamming. He turned. Three men. He could tell their walk. Hear the change. Three Birddogs.

"Two tickets," he said to the man in the booth.

"To what?"

"Two tickets. Seven o'clock train to New York."

"No New York train leaving this morning, son."

183

Blake glanced at his mother. "No. You don't understand. Now, two tickets for the New York train. I got cash." He opened his wallet.

"We got one boarding now for Miami. One to Washington at three-thirty P.M. tomorrow and one to—" Blake pulled Jess through the gate and ran down beside the new track. A line of silver cars. Ten or twelve people holding sacks and small bags.

Jess squatted down, shaking her head.

Blake looked down the rails. He felt his heart skip. Jess was sobbing. He set a hand on her head. "Now . . . Mama. Hush."

He sat down beside her. Held her hands. "Now, you don't cry. You . . . you get yourself settled now." He kissed her cheek.

The mascara was running down her face.

Blake put her hands between his thighs. "It's alright. It's no matter. You're tired. You got the train schedule mixed up. That's all. We'll still get it. You wait and see."

Jess shook her head again.

Blake felt himself beginning to weep. He had no strength to stop. "Come on, now. You tell me a joke. Let me see them eyes. Show me some pretty."

"It was something I thought you understood so well. You've got the same blood in you. All your life you've seen how I am. We are. It was comfort. Chasing. Hide and seek. Oh, I thought you were having fun, too."

Blake pulled her head against his chest. "You know, you're right. I never could—I never did get those logs to fit together. Just couldn't figure it out. I got confused. I confuse things and forget so damn easy. Just tell me now. When's the train coming? We'll come back for it. Just what time, Mama?"

She wept very quietly now. She spoke wiping tears from her mouth. "There's not one today. There never was one."

"Oh, God," Blake said. He let go of her hands.

"I'm sorry, baby. Mama's sorry."

"No train today at all?" Blake asked, closing his eyes.

Jess pulled his thighs back to cover her hands. "I didn't know you. I didn't know my baby. I'm sorry. Sorry."

Blake set his lips just beside her ear and hugged her closely. He whispered very slowly, deliberately, "There's no play waiting in New York for you?"

He felt her nod her head. A sound came out of his chest. He rocked her in his arms.

The rattling of the dimes brought him back. The Birddogs were moving closer. He kept one arm around Jess and, using his other hand, wiped mascara from her cheeks.

"I can take care of you, Mama. Let me do it. Please."

"You don't know how. Only the doctors know how. Only Cross."

"Uncle Cross?"

"He loves me. He knows all about me."

Blake felt a tremble in himself. A curve of cold across his ribs. He brought her hands together and kissed them. He touched her eyes and rose.

"I know. I see now, Mama. It's nothing against you. I understand. I love you. Come on. Get up now."

"Where?" Jess asked, her hands fallen to her sides, her head drooping down.

"We'll go to Miami. We'll get out of here."

"Can't."

" 'Board!" yelled the conductor.

"You love me. I know that. You love me now. There's not a minute of doubt in me about it. Please get up."

"I need to rest. I need to go back to the doctors who know me. They can give me medicine there. They can take care of me."

A car swept up beside the ticket booth. Cross stepped out lightly.

Alfbender jumped from the driver's seat. He ran forward a few steps.

"Get the hell away, Blake! Beat it!"

The conductor shouted for last passengers.

Jess saw Cross approaching. She caught hold of Blake's hand and stood up beside him now. "You get on that train. You do what Alfbender says."

Blake saw the Birddogs moving toward him in blurs.

"Blake, take it easy, son. You're sick. Let me take you home now," Cross shouted.

The train was pulling away.

Blake felt everything going down in his head. He looked at his mother. He tried to focus her face. "Mama, come on. You have to go."

He felt her body shove into him then, drive him toward the last passing door of a car.

"You get on!" Jess shouted. "You get your ass on that train!"

She kissed him, broke the amulet from her neck, put it into his hand, and pushed him onto the Pullman's steps.

Blake felt himself fall into the moving car. His legs still dangled. He looked out to see his mother running beside the track. He could just make out the changing of her face— from laughter to tears and back again. He saw the green eyes and high cheekbones and lovely mouth. He heard her voice just before the Birddogs caught her.

"Go on! Race! Run! Mama sees. Mama understands. I love you! I love you out there. . . ."